Stories

From A Whisky Bar

by

ralfy

Published by Irish Sea Trading Company Ltd:

Ramsey, Isle Of Man IM7 1HG

© Copyright Irish Sea Trading Company Ltd:

Stories From A Whisky Bar
First Edition

Warning – If you choose to drink alcohol, and are of legal age to do so in your Country of residence, drink in moderation and with consideration.

Know your healthy limits for the sake of yourself and also for those around you.

This book is a work of fiction. Any similarity to persons and situations in real-life is purely coincidental.

Condition of Sale

ISBN 978-1-9162575-3-5

Book edited by Barbara Harris.

Chapters

Prologue

... In 2019 I wrote a book called 'Search For A Whisky Bothy' to celebrate ten successful years as an online whisky reviewer with my YouTube channel called 'ralfydotcom'. The book was primarily autobiographical in content and told the story of my first experience as a child tasting my first whisky when I raided my dad's drinks cabinet, thereafter, developing an interest and taste for the stuff as an adult living and working in Glasgow. Even as that book morphed within my imagination and out of the reference photos I examined, I rapidly identified many interesting anecdotes and situations for contribution to that first book.

So much so in fact, that I exceeded the content needed to complete one book and had several chapters left, noted, archived, and yet to be written. These chapters are the foundation for this book, a fictional sequel, and different, in being an accumulation of separate, self-contained short stories, one per chapter, which make up this book.

I hope you enjoy it, it's personal, singular, and covers many aspects of my whisky-experiences, some chapters are simply fine old stories heard in bars, some just the embodiment of experiences I have had, and some are recreations of stories heard from others in the Glasgow whisky community.

I recommend a small dram of scotch to accompany each chapter.

When consuming whisky, possibly whilst reading this book, please keep it quality, not quantity, and please don't get pished and hurt yourself, it's not worth the hassle.

May the malt be with you malt-mates.

ralfy.

Hoochinoos.

A tale of friends enjoying a special evening of entertainment and human business somewhere in a quiet corner of Scotland.

Ruraigh much preferred to be called Rudy, it was a reggae thing, first discovered then delivered all the way from the sunny Caribbean through the radio, late at night, when less-popular and more specialist music was featured by the B.B.C.

A fine old valve wireless set sat in his front room on the wall opposite the fireplace. Resplendent in its art deco glory, a well-crafted, wood-fronted, sunburst-style thing with two speakers laying compactly side by side presenting a quality and solidity rarely found in modern appliances.

Bought at a negotiated price of only five pounds at a garage sale a few years before, Rudy had fallen in love with the eccentricities of this purchase a proud, shabby, period-piece which still actually worked, a miracle given its general condition and age.

The small modern transistor version it replaced was relegated to the back of the garage under an old tea towel to keep the dust off it.

As the winter slowly receded with the onset of spring, Rudy felt his spirits rise.

The awkwardly stocky, red-haired, warm-hearted neanderthal looking man in his late thirties found plenty of work with local farmers at this time of year, helping with the lambing and silage-scattering. It was a simple life, basic but with space to breath, and this suited him.

A small, isolated cottage at the foot of the Ettrick Glen provided a discreet, detached base in which to live more quietly.

The rent was low, the company limited but of good quality, and, after finalising his divorce, a much-appreciated place to recover from the bruises of a soured relationship.

Dennis had been a big help.

Rudy's best friend for a while now, Dennis had a naively cheery disposition, and did nothing to judge, or to offer too much help. He was just there as and when Rudy needed him.

The legal fees destroyed Rudy's savings. The divorce settlement destroyed his future plans, so it was with some trepidation that he arrived on the Island with no more than a brief seasonal contract with some local farmers, and nowhere to stay. Nowhere that is until Dennis phoned a friend.

Rudy was accepted by the community, settled in immediately, and was never really out of work from his arrival. Slowly and steadily he fell in love again, not with a woman this time but with the Island and its landscape.

With winter on the wane, Rudy sensed the time was ripe for a gathering of the Hoochinoos, and it was his task to make it happen. The previous meetings had been very successful, a quality social event come bonding ceremony of a small group of misfits who happened to be friends.

Rudy made the calls, ticking off the names as he went down the list scrawled in pencil on the back of a bus timetable. Dennis, Bobby, Tarq and Annie all confirmed attendance on the allotted date, which gave those that needed it a couple of weeks to deal with travel arrangements, . . . ferry booking and the like.

It also gave Rudy time to get a brew started.

The brew required some experience, skill, and a significant quantity of discretely acquired ingredients, accumulated over several months from diverse sources so as not to attract public attention. Dennis and Bobby being locals, helped in the requisitioning of 'stuff', although it was Rudy looked after sourcing the yeast, which was of particular importance.

By the garage, Rudy rinsed out a couple of thirty litre white plastic buckets with water from the hose pipe and thereafter placing the tubs inside and against the south wall of the garage, where it was warmest for drying. Two brewers electric heating pads were place under the separate tubs and plugged into sockets above. These would assist in maintaining the temperature of the tubs in case the ambient temperature fell too low. Four catering sized tins of prunes were opened carefully and divided between the tubs. Bags of sugar were dissolved in hot water in a large steel pot on the gas stove. The gas ring burned fiercely for over an hour to ensure that all the grains of sugar were completely dissolved before the syrup was added, still hot, to the tubs. In all twenty-four one kilo bags of granulated sugar were used for the purpose.

Rudy tasted the cooling but still steaming wort, thought a bit, then added two bottles of lemon juice recently bought at the local Co-op supermarket, one to each container. At this point each tub was three quarters full. He then retrieved a metal bucket from a corner in the garage and, removing the cloth that was draped over the top of it, examined its contents. A soft bloom of mould covered the brown soup in the pail. This was neatly scraped off and the residual content split evenly between the tubs. Back in the kitchen, a large sachet of yeast, ordered through the post, was carefully examined, opened and sprinkled into a plastic jug of prune juice and warm water.

"Coobra" the green and red packet said. 'Turbo yeast 48 Extreme', and above, at the top of the packet in smaller print, 'extreme up to 21%'. That of course meant twenty one percent alcohol if the temperature was kept consistent and enough sugar was present in the tubs. Rudy continued, examining at length the dissolving creamy-coloured yeast as it started to gently foam and come back to life within its new environment. Even if the outside temperature was low, there would still be a decent yield, such was the durability of the "Coobra". Bread makers yeast had been tried in the past, but the results were not the same. This turbo yeast delivered much better results.

After about a week, the tubs were checked, and all was well. Most of the sugar was now alcohol, light tasting and slightly fruity, dry and a little bitter.

Purely on taste, Rudy calculated that his wash was now at sixteen percent alcohol, any higher and the end product would be a bit too vodka-ish.

The weather had been kind over the week, so the results were good and only needed a little fine tuning. This came in the form of a touch of cider vinegar, along with some assorted spices - cinnamon, clove, cardamom and vanilla pods. The concoction was then left to its own devices for the following week where it could 'settle' prior to the meeting of the Hoochinoos.

Dennis assisted a couple of days before the get-together to help with the set-up in the kitchen which was useful as the still was rather heavy for lifting single-handedly onto the gas stove. At a sixty-litre capacity, it was weighty for its size, having originally been a heavy-duty copper hot water immersion heater, a discarded item from a demolished Victorian villa, gutted, inexplicably, by fire a decade previously. There had been rumours, but then all went quiet when the owners disappeared suddenly off the Island.

Dennis was a cheeky, wiry dark-haired man in his forties. Like Rudy, he had been through a harsh and messy divorce, so when the two first met in a bar down in the town, the rapport was immediate and sincere.

It was local-man Dennis who introduced Rudy to the cottage, to the farmers who provided seasonal work, and to the community, who, with Dennis's endorsement, accepted Rudy without judgement or scrutiny. Rudy was loyal, rewarding Dennis's friendship with his ability to provide eccentric conversation and good company, keeping positive when Dennis started getting negative about this, that, and whatever. The two even started to look similar, despite Dennis being a lot slimmer and slightly taller than Rudy. Both wore basic functional clothes, locally sourced, and Dennis even adopted Rudy's appreciation of Reggae by growing dreadlocks, which were mostly hidden away under a stretch-hat of dark grey wool. This was a topic of much mirth and hilarity. The art of growing and maintaining dreadlocks is not so easy until you know how. Most of what Rudy had learned about grooming from pals in Glasgow was applied to Dennis, but even after two years, he was still sporting mini-dreads. Rudy's russet locks went down to his waist as a result of ten years of carefully managed hair growth and grooming. His, overtly red, bushy beard completed the look.

Despite appearances, neither of the friends were actual Rastafarians, they just loved the vibe, the look, the music and culture, the Caribbean, sunshine, tropic Islands, the whole attitude.

'Shootin' the breeze' was what they called their monthly music and culture nights. Nobody else was ever invited to these home-gigs. They would sit and discuss Jamaica and the blue, blue water, . . . but for all the talk it was a place they had never visited, and they had no ambition ever to go there. The reality of it would have tarnished the beautiful dream.

The immersion heater had not converted successfully to a still in the beginning. The results being a bit too watery and anaemic. On the advice of a distiller down in Campbeltown, an angle grinder made light work of removing the unsuitable pot still column which was replaced with a copper dome made up from an old cauldron which was adjusted and welded into place with a descending copper-sheet lyne arm which was also added to assist condensing flow, and to look the part too.

It was a fine-looking still on completion, and after seasoning with some vinegar and boiling water, it worked a treat. After sampling the results for character, the proportions of the still was carefully measured and found to be 'proper third'd'!

The night before his guests arrived, Rudy settled into the cottage for the evening with the still balancing on the stove, and the cold water tap at the sink providing coolant via an old hosepipe into a white plastic home brewers tub below, the rather irregular coil of twenty two millimetre diameter copper pipe wound down from the lyne arm extension and eventually appeared through the wall of the tub at just the right height to pour condensate directly into a collecting pail of galvanised steel. Attempts to seal the wall of the tub where the pipe protruded had never really worked, so a modest leak of cold water onto the kitchen floor was accepted as a minor inconvenience. A small table stood nearby containing several glasses, a jug of water and a bottle of Irn Bru soda drink for those who wanted it as a mixer. Also, a chipped ceramic plate held an unopened packet of shortbread and oatcakes. Three demijohn single gallon glass bottles stood like soldiers along the back of the sink up on a shelf.

After an hour's preparation, the arrangements were completed in the kitchen and the still had been fully charged with fifty litres of mildly warm fermented wash from one of the plastic tubs in the garage. Having shut all the curtains and switched off unnecessary lighting, Rudy lit the gas stove and slowly heated the still to facilitate a good first-take of low strength spirit. This would be a slow process taking around six hours to complete. No gauges or thermometers were used, it was all done by sight using knowledge and experience. No gadgets were necessary.

The process was a game of patience, being attended to methodically, and with routine vigilance of the gas flame in relation to the hissing coming from the hot wash in the still, to the resultant steady trickle of spirit out of the pipe at the end of the cooling process. The rate of water flow from the kitchen sink was important, and any variance would either slow the run, or over-stimulate it and risk production of hot liquor. It was prudent to stand back now and again just to over-view the whole process and balance the gas flame heat against the flow of the distillate into the steel bucket.

After about five hours, Rudy adjusted his hat, and tasted the run again from below the cooling pipe, it was much lower in alcohol strength now and becoming 'frisky', so he now had his three gallon jars of 'good stuff' of about thirty percent alcohol, and the remaining run became feeder for adding to the next first-run in about a week's time. This feinty solution was cloudy to look at, sort of liquid grey but it often improved in quality if kept in a warm place prior to addition to the next batch.

Adding the three jars of 'good stuff' back into the, now drained and cooling still, another full gallon jar of previous run was sourced and added. Thereafter, the still was now topped up to half-full with more assorted 'good stuff'.

The water supply and gas was again checked that it was securely shut off, ready for the following night.

The next room to prepare was the front room. It was the largest room in the house, where most of the space was taken up with an old edwardian sofa, rather worn, but clean and well structured. Along with a few folding chairs, all was arranged to face the fireplace, the genuine centrepiece of the home, having been originally installed when the cottage was built over one hundred years previously. It was a characterful installation, sturdy and functional, an iron-blackened stove with a generous hob, and even the roasting spit hook remained suspended inside the chimney, still able to hold iron pots over the flames below. An inbuilt boiler was entrenched behind the lower part of the chimney allowing water from the tank in the loft to be heated without using any electricity, and thus making full use of otherwise wasted fire heat as it passed up the chimney and out into Glen More.

It was a cosy room, made cosier with the addition of a plastic palm tree standing seven feet in height, in the corner, beside a tropical sunset, painted brightly onto the wall in bold shape, and colours. Beside this artwork stood the sideboard with the wireless set and a cocktail shaker surrounded by paper straws, a plastic steel ice bucket and matching tongs.

Dennis would drive over early, carefully parking his van to obstruct entry to the cottage by any other vehicles. Wee Bobby, an accidental friend of Rudy and Dennis, would be arriving around mid-afternoon, pushing his bicycle with one hand whilst holding on to a dog leash, at the end of which was an ageing and rather crumpled brown border collie dog named Dash.

Dash had been adopted by Rudy to save the dog from being shot by one of the local farmers as the beast was of no use at working the sheep. Dash had a lot of character, but was hyper, and as such needed more activity than Rudy was prepared to provide. Bobby's assistance had been very welcome. He would often take Dash for a whole week seeing as he was not allowed a dog of his own due to his mosaic downs syndrome. As an energetic young man in his early twenties, with little prospect of real employment, Dash gave Bobby a mission, and they were becoming inseparable.

Bobby ignored his rather short, squat stature, and remained untroubled by his personal circumstance by way of a constant stream of activity and perpetual optimism. Bobby was also discreet, and generally kept himself to himself. His mother was happy with that. Despite advancing years and a repeat-prescription habit, she did just enough in looking after Bobby to keep the Social Care Department at a distance.

Bobby grinned as Dash pushed him aside and crashed into the house barking and tail-wagging like fury. Outside the front door, the poorly balanced bicycle crashed onto the cobbles having rolled off its flimsy side-stand again.

"Shoosh Dash, just shoosh a minute," snapped Rudy, slapping down the dog as it bounced up to lick his face. Bobby laughed, "He likes it here, but still wants to be with me, anyways".

Dash calmed down at the sound of Bobby's voice and trotted into the kitchen for the food that was yet to be put down to him.

"Tarry's comin' tonight, aff the ferry wi' Annie, they are meeting at Glasgow and getting the bus down to Wemyss Bay for the boat," continued Bobby, "I can take Dashy for a long walk, tire him out for tonight mebbies?"

Rudy nodded consent, aware that it will afford him some extra peace and quiet before the night commenced properly.

Three hours before the guests were due to arrive, Rudy made a cup of tea and lit the gas under the still, then sat down to enjoy the silence.

Bobby and Dash headed down to Ettrick Bay to watch the sun go down and to see the approaching rain clouds rolling ever nearer from across the Atlantic, all the way from the Caribbean, allegedly.

As the copper still began to hiss and rumble with the heat, a van could be heard grinding its way up the loose blaze of stones that formed a driveway to the cottage. Three, very different, people disembarked. Firstly Dennis who offered a cheeky two-fingers salute towards the kitchen window, knowing that Rudy would be watching. The second character was a worn out, but fit-looking, athletic man with dirty fair hair, cut short and swept back. He wore some ex-military gear, primarily a trench coat and baggy camo-pants, looking like what he was, an army officer who has recently left the forces. Clearly the forces were yet to leave him. It was unlikely to ever happen.

There was a loud squeal inside the van from a small, petit woman, looking younger than her forty years, thanks to the liberal use of cosmetics and the dress code of a much younger generation. Tight ripped jeans, and a short pink over-sized puffa jacket, of a shade that perfectly matched her blusher and lipstick. Her painted nails concluded the pink theme. Now, both her hands were pushing back a wave of long, curly black hair. "Ma' nail, my damn nail's just come off on that 'effin door handle," she complained, then laughed "but I can stick it back on, so you got any glue Rudy?" she suggested, waving her damaged nail-hand to keep the focus of attention briefly on herself. "And, by the way," she added, "Will we be getting to see you with your hat off tonight?"

"Ooooh" commented Dennis, "Now that would be a treat worth waiting for."

Whilst the still continued to gather heat, the kettle next to it provided fresh boiled water for the four mugs of tea now surfacing on the kitchen table. "sugar anybody?" enquired Rudy, "Yes, . . . one for Annie, two for me and four for Tarry, but don't stir Tarry's 'cos he doesn't like it too sweet," replied Dennis.

The three sat down in the front room and caught up with each others news as the teas cooled, and the copper still continued to hiss and rumble through in the kitchen. Dennis was the first to finish his, and nodding to the others, headed outside to move the van down the drive to more effectively block the entrance.

They will not be getting disturbed.

The hoochinoos are meeting now, and the outside world is not invited.

Night has arrived along with the rain, and two wet figures appear from down the road, one pushing a bicycle, the other trotting energetically alongside with his tail at a lop-sided angle.

Bobby and Dash are made a fuss of as soon as they enter, Annie throwing her arms around the lad and demanding a big kiss. "Is Dash no getting a big kiss too Annie?" demands Dennis, grinning. Everyone looks to Dash who's doggy-shocked expression causes a collective outburst of laughter. Annie dutifully blows Dash a kiss, then the Team shuffle through to the kitchen for the opening ceremony.

Five glasses have been placed on the kitchen table along with a large glass jug of fresh tap water.

Bobby is tasked with bringing through a bottle of Co-operative white rum of the brand name 'Admiral Benbow'. Labelled as a 'superior tot' and presented in a screw-top bottle at thirty-seven and a half precent volume alcohol. It is evenly poured by Rudy, slowly, and with precision.

Bobby gets a glass of soda as he hates the taste of alcohol, except when with his pals on nights like this, but he does not drink much, it's for the best!

As Tark is considered the most educated and eloquent, he delivers the opening ceremony toast.

"Here's to us, here is our toast,

Friends who meet as hoochers

and with this toast we make the most,

of being such modest creatures.

We may be fools,

We may be dumb,

but we will now be fearless

let spirit flow,

fresh from the still,

with night our only witness."

Tark finishes to a round of applause from the group, and Annie squeals in delight.

Dash starts barking. "Shut it, ya' wee mutt" shouts Rudy. "Or your going outside into the garage."

Dash goes silent, and scuttles off into the front room to lay down by the fireplace.

"You say the toast so well Tark, what with you being a bit posh and educated," chips Annie with appreciation.

"Yeah, he's good at that sort of thing," adds Dennis.

Tark raises his glass, in such a way as to suggest they all do so together.

Everyone obliges, and another toast is proposed.

"To us, to all of us, and to the Hoochinoos!" he declares.

"To the Hoochinoos!" proclaim the friends together, and loudly.

"Is that still nearly boiling yet Rudy?", asked Tark

Rudy checks, and finds from a brief nosing of the condenser tube along with a feel of the heat along the lyne arm that first-collection is only five minutes away. Bobby gets agitated, as this is getting near his big bit in the ceremony. All five friends stare intently as the first drip of liquor drops from the condenser into the bucket below. All is silent in the kitchen as drop turns to faster drop, turning to trickle, then to more of a trickle.

Within a few minutes, as Rudy switches his experienced gaze from blazing gas burner to condensed liquor flow, he nods approval to the friends. Bobby is gestured forwards by Rudy, and having been given an old teacup by Dennis, collects the first pour from the still.

Once half-full, he lifts up the cup, proclaiming,

"Not for us, just not for us."

Dennis joins in, "And who's that for Bobby, who's that for?", he asks.

"For themselves, just for themselves, so none for us for now", replies Bobby, aided by Annie, who keeps him right with the words.

"And who's 'themselves', who's 'themselves?", asks Tark.

"We do not know, we just don't know, because we need not know", responds Rudy.

At this point, Annie opens the back door leading out to the back, and Bobby, carefully carrying the teacup so as not to spill a single drop, shuffles over to the bushes by the garage and carefully deposits the vessel onto a cement bird bath stand. He does this slowly as it is important, and the rest are watching his every move to see if he dares to spill any.

He doesn't, all is well and after a stiff, quick bow to the bird bath, he returns indoors to where the light and the warmth is.

The kitchen is getting warmer now, and more tots of Admiral Benbow rum are getting poured.

"Of course, this stuff is not as good, but it makes the real stuff seem better," Annie declares, looking towards Rudy for direction on when the fresh spirit will be ready.

Rudy looks towards the wall clock, "thirty minutes till the flavour," he concludes.

"But we will catch some now though it's still a bit light," he adds, "so we can do our main ceremony."

This time, five glasses are filled with some fresh-make, and Bobby puts aside his soda to join in for the next toast. It will be his first and last sip of liquor.

The Five friends head outside into the rain-wetted night where the wind is now beginning to billow in the trees and ruffle the leaves of the evergreen bushes around the cottage.

Rudy leads this toast, as he is the still-master, and he therefore must. Tark pulls a compass from his pocket and using the light from Annies mobile, directs his stance to the West, shuffling left a bit to compensate from magnetic West, to true West.

Annie quips in, "Are you sure you've got Alaska yet Tarky?"

Once everybody has their bearings, all glasses are raised above heads. Rudy begins, -

"Here's to you,
you Hoochinoos,
we thank you for
your guidance.
We wish to state
we wish you well

and say that this reminds us,

- of all the hooch

you Hoochinoos

have hooch'd

o'er times, now timeless,

and with your help

we'll keep it clean

and so avoid the blindness."

"So let it be, and so it is," adds Dennis, raising his hand as if blessing the ceremony, then silently, with much dignity, the five friends salute their muse and empty their glasses of fresh-still'd liquor, tasting the flavours for some length before swallowing.

"Wow," exclaims Tark, "That, old chap . . . is bloody good stuff!"

Back in the kitchen, Rudy checks on progress and pulls a small jug of new spirit from under the condenser.

There is a hush around him as he re-fills the empty glasses and offers the jug of water to whoever wants to add some to the spirit.

Annie goes first, a ladies prerogative, and also because she likes the lighter, fruitier flavours, and is not shy about adding lots of water to cut the alcoholic strength.

"I'm just loving the fruity flavours here Rudy. . . did you use tins of prunes again to get the yeast started?"

Rudy nods, and heads over to the wireless set in the main room to get the music on, for the time has arrived for less chat and more sounds. It's a roots style of reggae, perfect for the mood, and Ronnie Davis sings through the speakers his acoustic version of 'Got to go Home'.

Annie holds her glass up and starts to sway gently, side to side. Dennis grins and gets a bottle of 'ghost ship' beer from out of the fridge before joining her for a shuffle. Bobby does his hand-sway dance in the corner, and Tark makes himself comfortable in a chair to watch the proceedings. He is not drinking much compared to the others as he does not want the intoxication to aggravate the subconscious memories of Operation Desert Storm. He lost many comrades to 'friendly fire' and thereafter lost some of himself too. This is never discussed. His small group of friends try to respect the situation.

"Hay, Rudy!" exclaims Annie, loudly, "Show us your dreadlocks" she demands. Rudy, by this time, is relaxing a little more, being now on his third bottle of 'ghost ship', so with Alpha Blondys version of 'Wish You Were Here' feeding through the wireless set speakers, he pulls his woollen hat off to let a good show of Celtic-red dreadlocks tumble down to his waist, thereafter he spins a little to get them moving, and everyone cheers their applause. Dennis spins a bit too, but with his locks being that much shorter, it just does not quite work the same.

"I would have thought that having a Jamaican mother would give you better dreads Dennis," quips Tark, somewhat sarcastically. Dennis just laughs off the baiting, and demands a dance with Tark.

To much laughter, Tark refuses, and leaps up from his chair to grab the plastic palm tree in the corner of the room proceeding to dance with it affectionately, and to a sudden eruption of laughter.

Rudy heads through to the kitchen to check the still, glancing first at the condenser flow, then at the gas flame, thereafter turning up the gas control lever just a little to accelerate the boil, just enough, but not too much. On checking the fresh collected liquor, he finds the flavour getting stronger as the alcoholic strength begins to diminish.

Sixty more minutes and they will be hitting the feints, the bit that Tark loves the most.

Dennis and Tark join Rudy to see how the still is doing, and three more bottles of 'ghost ship' are removed from the fridge.

"Annie is mixing some gin she brought with her into the liquor," remarks Dennis quietly, endorsing the three mens belief that they are true connoisseurs of this protocol, and somehow more authentic.

Tark tastes the spirit again, flowing gently from the still, "man, you really nailed it this time!" he pauses respectfully, "This must be one of the finest ever," he states, continuing to methodically nose his glass. Dennis nods approval, and Rudy accepts the endorsement.

"Prunes!" Rudy declares, "I used more tins of prunes this time to get the ferment going, *before* adding the molasses and bags of sugar. That sour-tub idea of yours Dennis was great, it's really worked, you can just tell the difference!"

The other two nod. "I added the sour-tub to the ferment near the end, and I think the extra acidity adds to the fruity flavour and depth," continues Rudy.

Tark sips again and nods his appreciation.

The three friends head back through to the bigger room to join the others and conclude their night of methodical intoxication and happiness.

The following morning, Bobby is the first to rise, and after feeding a hungry Dash, the two of them set off whilst the others continue to sleep off the previous night wherever they have found a comfortable spot in the cottage. Tark has slept in the garage on the floor.

The rain has stopped, the day is fresh, warm and clean. The road from Kilbride is downhill all the way to Kettrick Bay, and on the shimmering sands, and under the heat of the living sun, Bobby spreads his arms wide, feeling the warm fresh air blowing up the Kyle.

Bobby feels again the heat and brightness of the sun through his now closed eyes, and he lifts his head further to the sky, breathing slowly and deeply.

Life is good, and he is happy for being one of the Hoochinoos.

Drama at An Gearrannan.

- a tale of dramatic scenery, an old bothy, and a sudden personal crisis on the coast of Lewis in the Outer Hebridean Islands of Scotland.

My compact little Nissan Micra car is packed with warm spare clothes, a surfboard, a bag of smokeless coal, and about twelve assorted opened bottles of single malt scotch whisky, partnered with six Glencairn glasses, a simple glass tumbler, and a matching one litre water jug of a style guaranteed to pour properly in a controlled manner, and which will not drip inconveniently when replaced upright on a table.

Jugs that don't pour properly are a total waste of time and should not be tolerated.

All essentials are accounted for, and having been reassured by myself of my own preparedness, I hop into the driver's seat and set off out of Glasgow, via Perth and up the A9 towards Inverness on another big adventure.

The drive is a long one and taking up most of the day, but made all the easier by virtue of it being out of tourist season, and mid-week, so the long line of slower caravans expected with the weekend trippers are nowhere to be seen, and over-sized tour buses are not weaving at a snail's pace along more scenic parts of the journey. Tour buses tend to do a lot of their journey at a snail's pace due to the elemental beauty of the landscape, especially from Inverness to Ullapool along the A835, a majestic, meandering asphalt tributary linking the northern highlands to the outer Islands by virtue of the CalMac ferry which runs from Ullapool across the Minch to Stornoway on the Isle of Lewis.

Ullapool is a small and remote village consisting of around one and a half thousand inhabitants, poised on the rugged coast where salt-sea blasts meet rain-soaked rock and vibrant green turf. It is home to a rather good fish and chip shop called 'The Seaforth', where the chips are good, and the freshness of the battered fried fish is outstanding.

I enjoy a filling lunch outdoors on a bench with a coastal view, whilst the rain remains off for a few brief minutes and the sun almost appears through the grey, compacted, drifting clouds.

The CalMac Ferry leaves Ullapool at 5.30pm in a modest, but not uncomfortable swell, and heads west across the Minch towards Stornaway. The crossing takes around two and a half hours during which time I pour over the ordnance survey maps I have packed into the rucksack and try to get my bearings as to the best surf spots around the Island in relation to the forthcoming weather patterns. This, with experience, tends to remain difficult to predict, and such are the variables of west-coast weather, that its wise not to plan more than one day ahead.

A young woman is sitting opposite me in the passenger lounge, sipping a bottle of peach-flavoured Bacardi Breezer and sobbing quietly into her mobile device. She frequently pushes back her long brown hair from her thin, sad face which at some point in the past may have been happy, but possibly not.

She leans towards the device sniffling silently, and quietly warbles her inebriated misery towards the person she has on the other end of the phone. Now and again she pauses to have a short and indulgent moment of silence infused with tears, self-pity and negativity. This routine continues for some time. I soon get bored being adjacent to her situation and turn my attention to some of the other passengers. There are not that many, only about one hundred or so, so I quickly whittle my attention down to the gossipy and under-dressed old ladies clad in light summer clothes which are unsuitable for the place to which they are going, and also, to a solitary man, tall, slim, muscular and with spiky dirty-blond hair, just short enough not to need anything more than a quick brush to keep its shape. His bearing is interesting, I guess him to be a military type, an officer of some sort, he is plainly and discreetly dressed and not once does he use a mobile device, but seems content to simply sit in his seat and wait for the voyage to conclude. He looks athletic and determined, so I imagine him to be on some sort of secret mission to communicate with aliens laying low in one of the west-coast caves which lie along the jagged coast.

Rumour has it amongst the surfing community that frequent 'sightings' have taken place on Lewis.

His very old-fashioned ordinariness makes him stand out from all those around him, dressed as they are in bright synthetic branded fabrics and white plastic shoes, each and every one ordinary and unremarkable.

The sun is still high in the sky as the boat docks into Stornoway harbour.

With the wind still brisk, the clouds have thinned, and the atmosphere seems warmer with the brighter light of some direct sunshine adding a sparkle to the air. The vessel is soon empty as vehicles and their passengers divide along the various tributary roads which lead out of the town and into the great wilderness beyond.

I slowly drive passed the pastel blue painted hostel in Kenneth Street that I stayed in on my last visit the previous year, and where my surfers sleep was uninterrupted on a Saturday around midnight due to the forced entry through a locked front door by local drunken trawler men, looking for a laugh, and to steal residents food from the kitchen. They failed in their mission due to the determination of Karla, the manager, a well-built and feisty dark-haired, gothic-looking Polish lady, who barred the trawler men's way at the top in the stairs with the use of a dirty wet floor mop which she swung and stabbed in their direction forcing them back down the steps and out into the road. Sleeping in the roof-space, I missed that whole show, which was probably just as well as one of the drunkards got lippy with Karla and ended up with a sore face. Then things kicked off down the road on the dockside as polish reinforcements arrive to sort things out.

I drive on out of Stornaway along the A859 road and suddenly the broader landscape appears in its stark, treeless, water-logged beauty. Suddenly I feel the sense of relaxation and enthusiasm that comes with temporary, and much needed freedom from the daily grind of City life and a hectic job. I feel the release from the 'real' world suddenly hit me, and I turn up my CD player which affirms my mood with the Electric Light Orchestra album, 'Out Of The Blue' blasting tunefully outwards through the open windows of my vehicle.

Suddenly all is bliss.

Surf, sky, fresh air, and whisky-nights.

Last time, I stayed at the little cosy, noisy, blue-painted hostel in Stornoway, but this year, at extra expense, I am staying somewhere very different.

My route this evening takes me to An Gerrannan, and to the black houses of Lewis, one of the most hauntingly beautiful places I have ever stayed anywhere in the world, a sympathetically restored historical hamlet hugging the shore on the northern edge of Europe.

It's almost dark by the time I arrive.

A fussily conversational, but pleasant middle-aged, dumpy lady by the name of Shiona who acts as caretaker, assists me in completing the paperwork of registration then guides me down a winding track to my allocated cottage. Once inside, she shows me a small bag of coal and peat blocks by the fireplace in the small sea-facing room, asks me a number of overly personal questions on my plans, displaying a well-known trait of nosiness by Lewis people.

Finally, she wishes me a good night, and disappears off up the darkening hill into the night amongst the surrounding cluster of rustic traditional cottages which make up the historic village.

Now, I feel rather tired, it's been a long day and as soon as the kettle is on, I stoke up the small fire box in the snug little sea-facing room at the end of the cottage and get a roaring wee fire going in the grate.

I leave my bags standing, unpacked in the bedroom, and settle instead into a simple but comfortable chair allowing my fresh brewed mug of tea to cool as I pour the first dram of the evening. Glenfiddich 12yo, always a good start to a whisky-session!

The tea cools quickly, my dram level in the glass drops quickly, then, quite suddenly I fall fast asleep, even as the orange flames in the fire box bring a proper cosiness into the room.

My dram remains unfinished on a table by the chair.

Outside, the wind whips up from the ocean, bringing cold spattering sea-salted rain in its hasty breeze which breaks silently onto the hard stone walls of the cottage.

Having never spent much time sleeping in an armchair, I have a remarkably comfortable night. Around seven in the morning, I suddenly awaken, totally refreshed, and head into the kitchen to put on the kettle. Whilst it heats-up, I examine the cottage in the light of the new day.

It's called 'Taigh Thormoid 'an 'ic Iain' which translates as 'The House of Norman' named after the crofter and fisherman who originally lived there from 1824 to 1900.

I grab my tea and head along to the bedroom to explore. It contains a double bed with a brick-red covered quilt, honey-pine cladding around the stone walls from floor to waist height, and a small skylight providing just enough light to see by. It is very cosy and compact, almost cramped for space, but not quite. The kitchen is basic but competent and has genuine charm in its simplicity. The snug room is the star of the place, being just a bit too small, super-cosy and with a window opposite the fire-box, allowing a view to the shore where Atlantic swells break hissing and grinding onto rounded pebbles and jagged rocks.

I pass through the small, undersized front door, painted brilliant gloss white and of sturdy construction, onto a gravel path surrounded by clumps of turf and moss. The building itself is of dry-stone wall construction, the walls being five feet deep and of compacted turf in the centre for insulation and longevity. The stones are woven together like a tapestry, symphonic grey and inertly alive within the location. White-painted window frames are small, tucked discreetly under substantial layers of thatch-hay which make up the roof, which in turn is held down with ship ropes on which large weight-stones are attached for better anchorage and storm protection.

It is beautiful in the blending of function and form within its location. It is an eco-house where the practicality of the distant past inspires me in the present.

The rest of the dozen or so hamlets lay strewn up and over the hill, clustered around a main single-track lane of grey blaze cinder which weaves like a stream between the buildings. All the houses are similar in style, some being bigger and longer, providing accommodation either for families or youth hostellers. One of the buildings acts as reception, shop and café, while another one acts as a museum for remembering yesteryear, complete with its weaver's loom and assorted rustic paraphernalia.

As I complete my daylight tour, exchanging pleasantries with other curious visitors, I notice the sky clearing, the wind falling away, clouds thinning, and a regular, well-formed swell appearing out on the ocean. I seize the opportunity and check my surfboard which is still strapped to the car roof.

Ten minutes driving north leads to one of the best surf locations on Lewis, Dail Mor, known for its regular, clean, sand-breaker waves all contained within a pristine bay of rugged desolate beauty.

Some other surfers are already there and riding the eight-foot rollers which let them 'catch air' as they ease up and over clean peaks of sea water carried in perfect clean-peeling breaks.

I join them, thankful for my neoprene wetsuit which keeps me insulated from the cold saltwater.

The sun shines, and I spend some time just sitting on my sturdy, eight-footer board, built for stability, letting the rolling water pass under me, whilst above me is the sun and sky, and around me the restless sea and coastline merging into an elemental meditation of one-ness.

It is special, and I feel alive.

Too soon, the weather changes, as does the behaviour of the incoming tide, and the swells start to mush-up, breaking the predictable patterns of seven row swells which have allowed me to pace my activity. I paddle for shore and jog up the sand dragging my now heavier board, reaching the car just as the first rain fall strikes onto my face. Having washed my gear in a local stream, I pack-up and drive off back to An Gerrannan for food and heat.

The cottage is calming, and safe from the growing storm outside, not a big storm, but big enough to appreciate the calibre of shelter I am enjoying. A meal is prepared and consumed with a big dash of 'hungry' sauce, then, as the fresh-lit fire crackles into life, I begin to methodically pour my drams. Glencairn glasses are lined up on a handy shelf next to my armchair, all in a row and all in order of consumption.

My first dram is, predictably, Glenfiddich 12yo, which is, from experience, always a good choice to begin with in any session. The next pour is Bunnahabhain 12yo, chosen as it's a non-peaty Islay with distinct character, and rumour has it that the 12yo has 14 to 15yo malt in the mix.

For some reason, people think all malts from Islay are heavily peated.

The third dram is a further change of direction and is a 15yo Dalwhinnie, a well-rounded highland malt with honey-complex and depth.

Three more are still to be poured. I rummage through the options, until I pull out of the box a bottle of Glenglassaugh 15yo cask strength bottled by Cadenheads, the Independent bottlers from Campbeltown. This one is very, very good, being a lighter, oak-delicate, and sophisticated event of long development and crisp finish. Bottled at 53.7%vol, it is natural colour, unchillfiltered and quietly complex.

Bottle five is another older dram, Adelphi-bottled Mortlach distilled in 1980, and bottled in 2000 at the age of 19 years, with a strength of 59.3%vol. This is nectar, a magnificent sherried Mortlach and old-school in nature.

Lastly, my sixth dram of the session will be Lagavulin, A Distiller's Edition option in a black box and distilled in 1980, bottled at 43%vol.

A fine finisher.

I stoke the fire, turn on my CD player with some Vivaldi for company, kick-back in my chair with one ear listening to the cold rain splattering the small windowpanes behind me, and nose the Glenfiddich. A few sips later, and the wind rattles more rain against the window, seemingly in frustration at my snug and cosy retreat from the elements. The cottage remains stoic in its presence. Warm, dry and secure.

Four hours later and I am gently drunk.

Not uncontrollably so, it has been a well-paced session, nothing spilled, and nothing wasted, every moment and sip enjoyed enormously, appreciated and duly respected. A refilled tumbler of water, as always, has been the perfect companion to the drams, which are not all finished. I stagger to bed and am asleep even as my head hits the pillow.

The next morning brings a very different day, such is the climate of the Western Isles of Scotland.

The wind has fallen to nothing, the rain is off, but a damp, warm and thick mist sweeps to and fro along the rocky coastline beyond the village.

I shuffle, yawning, down to the shore and peer into the gloom out at sea. The sea is becalmed, the swell is gone, . . . no surfing today.

Eating my porridge quickly, I finish my cooling mug of tea and make a decision on what to do under the circumstances. Pondering the options, I check the weather forecast with Shiona up at the reception cottage, as local knowledge offers the best forecast for further surfing. She has a visitor, the blond-haired, athletic man I saw on the boat coming across to the Island. They are chatting softly as I enter her office but stop suddenly as soon as they become aware of my presence. Whilst Shiona remains distracted by my sudden appearance, I take the opportunity to say a cheerful 'hello' to the blond-haired man. He reluctantly introduces himself as Tarquin, he seems distant, troubled almost, and takes control of our brief conversation with small-chat about migrating birds and ornithological stuff, and he seems reassured now to have clearly explained his reason for being there, but I'm not sure I believe him.

We exchange a few more simple pleasantries, and then I get my longer forecast which, reassuringly, suggests a good swell for the following day. I turn to leave, and as I do so, notice a map half-closed and slid to the side on a table between Shiona and the man. It is not a normal, ordnance map of the 1:50,000 scale and with a pink gloss cover, this is different, green cover, sepia images, suggesting a scientific reference.

I politely leave, pausing at the door, perchance to hear a snippet of their conversation.

Both remain silent and I move off after a few seconds.

Back at the cottage of Norman, I finally make up my mind as to how to fill the day meaningfully, and put on my running shoes. I head outside, take a deep breath of warm, salt-laden air, and do a few kicks to warm up and stretch before jogging off down to the beach, before suddenly taking a swift right turn and heading up the green, mossy slope, strewn with the rubble of fallen old cottages, where I clamber up the costal path which leads north to the cliff tops.

The air is remarkably warm, the wind is still, and the atmosphere is beautifully fresh, enriched with ozone. The landscape is like a saga, jagged ancient rocks embedded within soft ultra-green, springy turf, lush, and damp. My trainers spring on the soft surface, and it makes for easy running, even uphill.

The cool Atlantic mist continues to billow thick and wispy, threading unevenly over the mounds of turf and rocks, creating a surreal atmosphere of other-worldliness which spurs me onwards, upwards, up the hill, past small cairns of stacked stones, left as numerous hillwalkers legacies over the years and accumulating into perfect mounds, stacked high into cones of grey rubble.

I run from one to the next, using them as markers, whilst in the mist I hear the sound of waves and gulls. In the distance I notice a choice of two cairns, a smaller one to the right, and a much larger one to the left, and stationed a little further away. I trot briskly up towards the bigger cairn, further up the slop of grass, the thick mist weaving ever more tightly in front of me as I gather pace.

Suddenly, a stern voice inside me commands that I stop running.

It is a shock, and my heart races at the loud command within me. I slow, then slow down some more, even as the tall cairn looms attainably into view. Again, a voice commands me stop, loud and invisible within me.

I reluctantly stop, wondering what is happening to me. . . some hallucination or something.

Walking forward a few steps, the mist suddenly clears with the rush of salt-laden air blowing vertically up the deep cliff edge in front of me, I am only two feet way from a sheer drop of over one hundred metres down onto blackened jagged rocks below, glistening in the foam of ocean breakers, crashing, white and angry. Looking up, I now see the tall cairn in front of me, only about twenty metres away and perched on top of a tall, narrow needle stack of rock, surrounded by foaming seawater.

My legs begin to tremble uncontrollably as I throw myself backwards into the safety of some wet green turf.

I lay there trembling, a clear vision of my broken body laying between sea and rock, smashed and lifeless, playing before my eyes. I have very nearly died, but am still alive, and now experience the aftershock of the event.

I lay there, where I have fallen, wet and shivering in the mist, the silent air, and the sound of distant crashing waves a reminder of my narrowly avoided fatality.

Hugging into the solidity and safety of the earth, I lay motionless, dizzy, numb and in some shock.

After a few minutes, and after the trembling has subsided, I roll over onto all fours, and I crawl on hands and knees further away from the cliff edge, to the reassurance of greater safety, and a better chance of seeing the sun set on another day.

Walking slowly inland a little, I breath more deeply than I need, as it feels like the best thing to do.

After a while I find a wet and soggy path over the Fivig Burn which weaves lazily on its way towards the cliffs, and arrive at the cairn above Loch Sgairbheiseal where I begin to feel a lot calmer.

It's downhill now heading North West again and soon I see the golden sands of Dail Mor, peaceful, calm and deserted, except for a solitary figure within the confines of one of the small cemeteries which sit in two parts either side of the stream, meandering down and into the bay.

As I get a little closer, I see that the figure is that of Tarquin, who I had met earlier at the village, I raise my hand to give him a wave, but he does not respond, and seems, in fact, not to even notice me.

Rather than interrupt, I sit for a while on the shoreline and contemplate further my brush with death, how ironic to consider this whilst sitting between two cemeteries.

I notice after a while, as I turn around to check, that he has moved away now and is heading back up the single-track access road into the distance. Out of curiosity, I venture to where he has been standing and discover a neat row of commonwealth military gravestones, standing to attention as if on parade. Laying neatly beside one of the stones is a fresh red poppy weighed down with a brass belt buckle, clearly old, and military in style.

I move away, it's now as if a change in the air is allowing me to feel normal again after my recent experience, and I head on up the single track road, inland, and up to the main junction of a safer road back to An Gearrannan, and back to the safety of Normans house with its' thatched roof, fireside and assorted bottles of whisky.

As I enter the village, the rain is returning, spattering violently onto the tarmac in the car park.

Shiona scuttles out from behind an outhouse clutching in both her arms a small lamb, no more than two weeks old. She nods me a cheery grin and shouts across for me to help her gather the other, larger lamb which has now escaped from the shed.

I willingly oblige, happy to be helpful, and despite weary legs from all the running and walking, I join her inside a dry-walled pen where a boisterous and clearly, independently minded mature lamb is running around enjoying the brief freedom from the captivity inside the shed.

Shiona tells me to chase slowly, and wave my arms wide either side, as I head-off the lamb up the small slope within the pen, which is the way they prefer to run, uphill, as is their instinct. After a few goes, I lunge and grab two back feet, not anticipating how strong such a small creature actually is. Before I know it, I'm on my face and sliding behind the lamb, still clutching it's back feet, and into a stack of peat blocks. I don't let go, and despite a mouth full of damp peat, I keep a hold on my prey, and find that grabbing its' woolly fleece seems to calm it down and render more passivity. The wee rascal stares at me belligerently, and then licks my face as I establish a better grip and lift it up into my arms.

Shiona, by this time, is laughing herself silly, being much entertained by the theatre of my assistance, and so too is Tarquin, now hanging over the wall, grinning from ear to ear like a cheshire cat.

We chat a bit, now that two small lambs have allowed an opportunity for conversation, and a few refreshing pleasantries are exchanged between the three of us. As Tarquin makes his excuses to leave, I notice him briefly look troubled, but then swiftly return himself to normal, for politeness. Shiona seems to see more than I do and gives a reassuring hand on his shoulder for a few seconds. The lambs are both now back in their pen, and I pull Shiona away from her conversation with him, requesting that she use my camera to take a few pictures of myself with the lambs, in their pen, for my album.

The lambs prove to be very adept at their modelling work, and after less than a minute, I have several good quality photos with the dry wall showing up well behind us, the peat smears still intact on my face and hands.

I look outside, but Tarquin is gone.

Shiona looks towards me inquisitively, lowers her voice, and tells me a little of his circumstances. He lives a strange life, affected by betrayal and shell-shock, but still working on various official projects.

I am told he has friends on the Isle of Bute who he finds to be supportive and understanding, but not much more is said. I slowly nod my sympathies, realising my own near-death experience on this day maybe somewhat pedestrian in comparison.

It's getting dark now, although it's still summertime and should be light till late, however, grey rain clouds are scudding swiftly in from the west bringing fresh storms and rain.

Inside Normans thatched house I feel instantly secure and warm, protected now from the elements, and safe at last from the drama of the day.

I make a cup of tea, nursing the hot ceramic mug in both my hands as I sit and watch the fire now crackle into life and spouting small sporadic orange flames behind the glass door of the stove.

I soon realise that I'm getting too comfortable too soon, so get up, and still holding the hot mug in both hands, head over to the front door, pause to set down the mug, open the door, and stand still observing the darkening, greying skies casting deep shade over the wild landscape in front of me.

I shiver.

I stare out a little longer, but not too long as the air is getting colder and giving notice of another temperature change revealed in the white-crested waves dancing like little white horses onto the wet and salted shingle which foams and rolls with the constant presence of the tide, in and out, forward and back, animating that small place between land and sea.

I cast my eyes up to the sky to be greeted by large cold raindrops hitting my face, making me shiver and blink. I take a step back from the threshold and immediately the warmth and cosiness of Norman's house envelops me, even more-so as I shut the front door firmly and having finished off my drink, I proceed to prepare some dinner of chicken and mushroom soup, fresh made and well-seasoned with herbs and spices.

Thirty minutes later, I am sitting comfortably, full up, by the fireside in the small room, listening to the increasing rattle of hard rain against the small low-set window which looks down onto, and over, the shoreline. The little white horses breaking onto the shore are bigger now, angrier and noisier. I pull the curtains across and settle down for a round of whiskies and music.

I am soon joined by an old familiar presence, my whisky spirit, one that appears in the moments that I am no longer sober, but not yet drunk.

Orlando the orange cat lays in the corner beside the fireplace, having just arrived from out of nowhere. I can hear him purring, he seems content. I pour another whisky.

I drink my Glenfiddich 12yo malt rather quickly and follow up it with another measure. The choice of music is not my usual, for some reason I pull out a CD of 'Spem In Alium' composed in 1570 by Thomas Tallis, and sung by a choir called 'The Sixteen'. I put on my headphones to increase the immediacy of the music, which, like the ocean swell beating onto the shore outside, unravels in increasing waves of melody and drama. I feel a few tears moisten my eyes as the experience of the day returns, prompted by the surging effect of the music. As soon as the piece is over, I listen to it again, but louder this time. I hear within the music my life and death as one, the people, the lambs, the place, the elements.

On pouring a third glass of malt, this time, Lagavulin, and a very large one too, I surrender to the day I have just had, now made surreal by the music and alcohol, morphing into something else, a presence of alchemy, unattainable to me except for the unique circumstances of the day.

My life, my near-death, sympathy for a stranger, stark landscapes, huge skies, gentle winds, weaving and winding white mists around the cliffs below me, and catching and then cradling the lambs, absurd in their innocence and vulnerability.

The first wave of intoxication arrives, gentle but telling, I drink some water, turn up the music to listen again to what I have just listened to, then pour more whisky, enough to quell the internal agitation of nearly dying, and horribly so, possibly never to have my body recovered if it had been swept from the broken, blackened rocks on receding waves, out into the ocean and beyond, my family and friends never to know what happened. Another 'missing' person. Gone without closure to the few who cared. I shiver violently, pray briefly to a better and more caring god, then drink until I sleep.

Tomorrow will be fine, some surfing, life, appreciated more than yesterday, and the day before yesterday. Tomorrow brings the rest of my life, and whisky will continue to be a constant companion.

Orlando the cat stretches his paws, blinks, and returns to sleeping by the fireplace.

I remain in the armchair, covered now with a blanket, watching the dying glow of the embers in the fire until oblivion finds me and brings me deep and dreamless sleep.

Ella.

- how two friends implement a dangerous plan to improve their quality of life, oblivious to the odds stacked against them by fate.

"Am tellin' you Pats, I'm just sick and fed up to my back teeth with that bastard!" raged Ella down the phone to her friend.

"It's happened again, ever since he retired last month, Sannys going into the pubs and bookies and spending a fortune on the horses, and we've not even paid the house 'aff yet!"

Patsy murmured some soothing, sympathetic tones down the phone without saying anything specific.

Ella started to sniff and sob, "I'm at the end of it Patsy, I just can't take anymore, I'm going to have to leave him, . . . before I kill 'im."

At this point Patsy interjected, "C'mon now dear, never commit yourself to anything in the heat of the moment ... get out in the garden ... have a cigarette and simmer-down," she reassured,

"We will meet tomorrow morning at the Tea Garden in Partick, you know the place, and have a blether, . . . Eleven o'clock"

She paused, "He's no hitting you, is he?" asked Patsy, more seriously.

"No, no-no, nothing like that," responded Ella immediately, "Just being useless, grumpy and nasty, especially now he's no longer working. ...at least that kept him occupied for most of the time," she paused briefly in thought, "He's a lot worse with all this extra time he's got right enough."

Patsy murmured sympathetically again.

Both women exchanged goodbyes down the phone.

Ella headed into the garden for a cigarette.

The rain was coming on again and Ella shuddered in the damp chill.

Shivering, she sought refuge back in the kitchen to finish her smoke and sort out a mug of tea.

The following day was still as cold as the previous, but with the rain having stopped, there was a freshness in the morning air that Ella appreciated as she walked along Dumbarton Road to meet Patsy in the Tea Garden Cafe.

Slim, elegant, though a little wrinkled, her thirty dutiful years of domestic 'bliss' were carefully masked with a generous use of loud cosmetics and bright clothes. Her long, greying, brunette hair was methodically groomed into the beehive style popular in the 1960's.

Ellas' appearance was a contrast of desire over reality which almost worked except for her skirt being just a little too short, her heels a little too high, and the amount of catalogue-sourced jewellery being a bit too much.

Patsy waved cheerfully though the cafe window as Ella trotted down Gardner Street.

Unlike Ella, Patsy took full advantage of her shorter, plumper shape by self-expressing in a carefully tone-matched grey and black woollen trench coat, which covered a mohair, roll-neck sweater over baggy dress trousers and finished with discreet designer trainers, giving off the message that she was active and very self-aware in terms of herself.

Her use of colour was restricted to an expensive scarf of gold silk embellished with small multi-coloured sequins. Patsy kept cosmetics to a minimum, and never bothered to wear any jewellery, ever. It was not her thing … she was more cultured!

The two made for quite a contradiction in appearance, but there was nothing contradictory about their friendship which had morphed successfully over recent years.

Tea and toast were swiftly ordered in the muted and charming environment of the café. It was a favourite location with the two friends, as it was reliably unpretentious and discreet enough for relative anonymity from gossip.

Ella removed a paper hanky from her handbag, sniffed and dabbed her eyes slowly and carefully, before proceeding, "It's just that time's going on and I feel trapped Patsy, just trapped in an endless cycle of Sanny's needs and indifference." she leaned forwards over the table, nearer to Patsy, "And it's now killing me!" she concluded, waiting patiently for a response.

Patsy stirred her tea and looked out the cafe window in contemplation.

"He's even worse without the whisky!", Ella added, encouraging a response from the still thoughtful Patsy, adding, "It's only when he's pished, that I get some peace and quiet."

Patsy sighed, removing her gaze from the window, and turned her attention to Ella, who by this time was threatening to display a bit more emotion than was considered seemly in a public space like the Tea Garden Cafe.

Patsy paused, thinking a little more, furrowing her eyes, and suddenly laying both hands firmly down onto the vinyl table cover, "Now, listen to me carefully darlin', I'm being serious here." she gazed directly at her friend to assure eye contact. "Every problem in life has a solution, and those who are strong create solutions, whilst the weak ones remain the victim of the problem for ever."

Ella listened in silence. The threatening tears held at bay in response to Patsys' sudden authority.

"I'm just saying darlin' this is not the time or place for the talk we now need to have, so how abouts we meet next week at the Art Gallery for lunch. We can sort some things out and make an action plan." she added, before concluding solemnly with, "Every problem has a solution, and the winners are the brave and courageous. Ella . . . do you hear what I'm saying to you now?" said Patsy, staring intensely at Ella, trying to gauge her friend's response.

"I think so Pats . . . I think I do."

Later that evening, Ella sat alone in her kitchen extinguishing another cigarette as Sanny fumbled with his key at the front door lock.

"It's OPEN," she yelled.

Sanny entered through the door slowly. A small, dumpy, muscular man, hair in a ponytail, thick horn-rimmed glasses, low over his reddened, swollen nose. He stumbled briefly, clutching the wallpaper with both hands as he passed the kitchen door, and without a word to Ella, headed down the hallway slamming the bedroom door behind him.

Ella paused, waited, listening attentively, but as Sannys bedroom was now silent save for sudden rhythmic snoring, she headed into the front room to watch Coronation Street on the telly. Thereafter, having extinguished her last cigarette of the day, she retired to her room upstairs, bolted her door, and having taken her sleeping tablets, went to sleep.

The next morning, Ella organised the weekly shopping list, sitting at the kitchen table and finishing off a second cigarette as the sun rose brightly over the rain-wet roof tops across the road. A sudden sadness made her shiver and a sense of unexplained loss brought tears to her eyes.

She quickly stood up and wiped them away, shocked at the realisation that the emotion was for herself, a sort of self-pity.

The following week brought a change in the form of warmer, brighter weather. Winter morphing into spring and blossom was now appearing on the flowering cherry trees, glowing bright and cheerful. The Art Gallery in Kelvingrove was enjoying a brief lull in visitors before the summer tourist season started.

Ella was clearly looking strained and more stressed than at their last meeting.

Although they both enjoyed the hustle and bustle of the Tea Garden cafe, it was Patsy's idea to try other venues for meeting-up, and as she considered herself artistic and cultured, the Art Gallery, which was also a significant museum, was chosen.

Ella found it a bit intimidating, but Patsy's affable pretentiousness as they walked around the place was entertaining and well-intentioned.

After a brief tour of the now familiar exhibiting rooms on the ground floor, the ladies headed towards the grand front hall where they made for a small metal table with two chairs which had been recently vacated in a discreet corner of the roped-off cafe area.

A couple of large cappuccinos along with two cream and raspberry meringues were ordered.

Ella insisted on paying, however as soon as she opened her purse, she quickly noticed that the paper money that she thought she had, was gone, and the remaining coins would not cover the total cost.

Patsy smiled sweetly at her friends predicament, and paid with her swipe card, much to Ellas' embarrassment.

As they stirred their coffee and cut the cakes into small, more manageable pieces, there was silence.

"Well then Ella!" commenced Patsy breezily, breaking the mood, "Are you going to tell me why your looking like you just got dragged through a hedge backwards?" she stared intently at Ellas' dishevelled face.

Ella looked away, preferring to acknowledge uninterested passers-by, rather than engage with her friend.

"Somethings just not right Patsy!", she paused, looking into her coffee, "I feel that I'm just fading away and dying."

Patsy sighed and rocked backwards into her seat.

"So that's it darling!" she responded, "You have finally admitted the existence of something you needed to know. Don't deny it Ella" she continued, "I know it when I see it, 'cos it happened to me, and it happens to others too."

Ella butted in, "But it's ok for you Pats, your man Alex died just at the right time. You didn't have to carry on with the divorce and all that upset."

"True …and it saved a fortune in lawyers fees," Patsy added with satisfaction, "But" and she lowered her voice, "That situation was not left in the hands of fate."

"What do you mean by that?" demanded Ella.

"I helped him on his way!" said Patsy.

Ella was confused, then swiftly the gravity of Patsys' statement hit her.

"Are you winding me up Pats?"

"No darling, I'm serious," There was a brief moments silence, "Ella, listen, I'm very, very serious."

It took a further few minutes for Patsy's sudden declaration to sink in, but even as Ella's thoughts struggled to contemplate the situation, recollections of Patsy's circumstances around the unexpected death of her late husband Alex came into focus.

"It's so much easier than you might think," continued Patsy, easing herself gently into a more comfortable position, "It saved my life, and darlin', it could save yours too!"

Ella looked across the table sharply, "Are you being serious here?" she gasped.

"Are you telling me I should bump off Sanny? . . . are you even being for real?" spluttered Ella, her voice raising in anxiety.

"Well, look at me now Ella, I have money, time, freedom, AND my life is mine." she paused for a reaction, "And how about you Ella . . . how exactly is your life, sweetheart?"

Ella felt something stir within. Several things actually, something dangerous, something sad, something angry.

They both stood up from the table, Patsy leaning across to give Ella a kiss on the cheek, "How about we have a wee sit in the park tomorrow Ella, the weather forecast is good and sunny,"

"Think about it!" she added a few minutes later, as Ella boarded a bus on the main road and headed back home.

That afternoon Ella thought about it, and in the evening, as Sanny staggered in through the front door, drunk and silent, Ella felt something turn cold inside her.

"Have you had a good day Sanny?" she enquired.

He ignored her.

"Have you been dipping my purse for my money again Sanny?" she enquired, her voice raised and trembling."

"You mean OUR money, . . . ya daft wummin," he replied sarcastically.

There was a moments awkward silence.

Ella paused, picking her words carefully, as Sanny stared back across the room at her.

"Sanny . . . . darlin' . . . how much are you spending at the bookies these days?" she trembled.

"Nothin' tae do with you . . . *darlin*," he spat, and slamming the kitchen door, strode out down the hall and off into his room for more whisky.

As Patsy had predicted, the following day was bright and warm as the two friends met in Victoria Park, at a sunny spot by the duck pond.

Patsy had thoughtfully brought bread for the birds.

"You see this Ella?" she stated, "Freedom, empowerment, I can do what I want to do, and not worry about money because I'm not reliant for it on someone else."

"Sanny earned good money as a cooper up in the warehouses at Drumchapel, what with all the overtime he was doing." She paused, "But do you see any of it, Ella?"

Ella remained silent.

"I helped Alex pass-on, but only because he was killing me darling." she paused again, thinking, as she scattered bits of bread over the pond for bird feed..

"His stupid investments pulled us apart, and I had to start divorce proceedings before we lost everything". "But that was not enough, and after I found out the extent of his 'weakness' I realised it was me, or him."

Ella stared across the water, shivering in the sunshine, "How did you do it then?" she asked calmly.

"Well, nothing sudden and obvious, so I took my time and fed him toxins. Weedkiller, painkillers, aspirin, paracetamol, Ibuprofen, crushed cherry stones, laxatives. . . anything from the chemist shops, building it up slowly, over time, adding it slowly, in low doses, gradually to his food and drink".

Patsy paused to consider more specific details.

"Then I arranged a trip to the doctors for him, he was diagnosed with stress and put on antidepressants," she smiled, "They really helped move things on when he went on them. His doctor helped me a lot, what with all the different drugs he prescribed"

Ella listened intently.

"Think about it" continued Patsy, "A sudden and violent *passing* will get the police at your door in hours, it's so obvious, but, why would anyone ever suspect a slow dea' . . er, *passing.* That circumstance gets noticed by no-one, 'cos it's expected you see, . . . don't you?".

Ella nodded, shivering again in the warn sunshine now sparkling off the pond water.

Patsy put her hand on Ellas arm, "Remember young Jean Skimming who lived in Maryhill?" she queried, "She was getting cheated on and humiliated by her man, so she stabbed him with the bread knife in a rage, and now she's in for ten years, an open prison, but even on early release, she's coming out to nothing, just nothing, and she will never get her life back, not now after the way she did it."

Patsy continued earnestly, "Whereas, take Senga McGregor, that sweet old dear round the corner from me, but getting hit by her man Walter 'cos his dementia was getting worse, and she had enough one day. and it was her family that supplied the cocktail of stuff that eventually did away with Walter. Her skill was to do it slowly over a year, steadily, gradually and to say nothing to anyone, ever. Once the doctors got involved, that was the end for him. It was relatively painless... not distressing to anyone, and now he's all but forgotten. Senga is off in Benidorm for half the year, with her grandchildren visiting her every few months. She got her life back," concluded Patsy,

"THAT'S how you do it! Have a good reason. Tell no one. Say nothing. Do it slowly. Take your time. Be methodical and patient." Patsy said, as though explaining to a child. "All you need, will be found in a chemist shop or garden centre, just don't go to the same ones too often. Then, involve the doctors later so they can prescribe more toxins by prescription."

Patsy rested back on the park bench where they were now sitting, leaving the peace and quiet of the park to converse with Ella who was deep in thought.

After a while Ella turned to look at Patsy, "You know Pats you're a real friend to me, and I appreciate your advice."

Later that day, and back in the house, Ella sat in the kitchen budgeting her weekly shopping and lighting up another smoke to keep her company for five minutes.

The room seemed more silent than usual, but she could make out the sound of activity in the garage at the end of her garden. Sanny must be having a rare day off from the pubs in Partick, and the bookmakers too, . . . perhaps he was barred again. He would be sitting on a stool behind his old car, writing poetry, something he always did on those rare, more sober days.

Ella found some paper and a pencil from above the fireplace and started to write herself a list, of risks in one column, and benefits in the other column …weighing the pros and cons of her husbands death. Eventually, after another smoke, she concluded that, if Sanny died, she would be able to pay off the mortgage on their home, get all his pension, sell his old bottles of whiskies laying around the garage, and go on holiday. A good holiday …one with luxuries.

She then went into the garden and burnt her list in the fire bin.

Ella phoned her intentions to Patsy who quickly told her nicely, but firmly to 'just shut up about it and keep quiet', which she dutifully did.

A little later Ella put a large pot on the stove and started preparing a stew; stirring the vegetables into the tinned tomatoes, lentils, beans, fresh minced beef, and flavouring the cooking pot with stock cubes for a richer flavour.

Arms folded she headed out to the garage.

"Sanny darlin," she enquired cheerfully, "Sorry I've no' been myself lately, it's my time of month and that winter-wipeout disorder too, so I am making a nice dinner for you." Sanny looked up from his writing bench, confused. "Oh, er, thanks Ella, I'll be over in a while to have my dinner then."

"Sanny," enquired Ella, "Do you still have the gardening stuff here in the garage?"

Sanny gestured to the tools and bottles in the far corner near the doors then focussed back to writing his poetry.

Ella moved across to examine the options, then lifted a proprietary green plastic bottle of concentrated weed killer and headed back towards the kitchen to stir the stew and put it on a simmer.

Sanny appreciated the unexpected attention and care over the next few months, Ella seemed to have changed a bit . . . was a lot less bitter than she used to be. Perhaps it was down to his worsening health, he was not feeling so good, perhaps it was a dose of that seasonal disorder.

Ella made more stews, and despite being a bit on the salty side, Sanny loved them, they had such a rich flavour, and allowed him to handle more of the whisky that he kept conveniently in a barrel salvaged from his time at the cooperage, although, he noticed as of late that the liquor was more 'chemically' than he expected, but it was not too much of a problem as he was not really bothered about the flavour anyway. In casks, especially in summer, he could expect the flavours to change as the wood exerted more and more influence, which was why he regularly topped up his own barrel with 'fresh' content provided by an old work mate.

"Are you ok darlin?" Sanny enquired one day, having just finished some very sweet porridge provided by his wife. He had glanced over as Ella finished stocking up the kitchen cupboards and had suddenly spotted the stacks of pharmaceuticals on the top shelf, along with a green plastic bottle from out of the garage.

"You've got enough to treat an army there sweetheart!" he added, awaiting a response.

"It's just fine Sanny," stammered Ella, caught out unexpectedly by his observation.

She thought for a second or two, still drying a plate by the sink, "Womans problems," she retorted.

Sanny said nothing more about it, but went silent, as if sensing something he was not aware of.

"I've not been feeling so well myself over the last month Ella,"

"You should go to the doctors Sanny, get checked out," she brisky replied. "I will make you an appointment!"

"So the doctor has told Sanny that he has liver problems, what with all the alcohol, and stress too, what with his lifestyle and such, so I need to keep an eye on him a bit more Patsy," declared Ella, stirring her cappuccino at the Tea Garden Cafe.

Patsy gave Ella a long and knowing look.

Finally, after placing down her cup and removing her gaze from the window, Patsy leaned across the table towards Ella, "Don't rush anything, just take your time, let the doctors prescriptions have their way," she stated authoritatively.

"What's he been given anyway?"

Ella looked thoughtful, then pulled out her list from the chemist shop.

"Anti-inflammatory, painkillers, anti-depressant, water tablets, statins, beta-blockers," she read from her list, "But his blood tests came back as typical for his age and condition."

Patsy smiled, nodding her approval at the situation.

"They will certainly help him." she said, matter-of-factly.

It all happened sooner than expected.

Sanny had been in the kitchen finishing his stew, looking pale, bloated and tired, he struggled to finish it.

"Ella darlin'," he paused, suddenly becoming emotional, "I have never deserved you," he said staring towards an uncomfortable Ella who was drying some plates by the sink. "You have been so good to me recently, and I don't deserve your loyalty for all these years, and I just want to say thank you for sticking by me, whe' . . . when you could have walked out and no one would have judged you for it, what with how I have been to you over the years".

Ella listened silently and gave no response.

She smiled quietly, went across the room, and gave Sanny a long hug.

"I love you Sanny, and I always will till the day you die."

"Thanks my darlin' Ella, I love you too."

Sanny went off to his garage, and Ella turned on the telly to watch Coronation Street.

By eleven o'clock she could see that the light was still on in the garage, and on checking, found Sanny lying face down on the floor, assorted coloured tablets laying around him like confetti.

An empty glass of water remained on the work bench, surrounded by sheets of recently written poetry and pastel drawings. She stood silently for a few minutes feeling numb and remote.

Ella had had a long day, so left things as they were, closing the garage door tight to keep flies out, and headed off to bed. The rest could wait till the morning when, refreshed, she would be phoning the doctor and dealing with the formalities.

The funeral was a simple affair. Patsy proved invaluable with helping to register the death and arranging the funeral. As she said, "I've done it all myself before anyway, so I know the script."

A couple of Sannys old workmates turned up at Clydebank Crematorium, along with a few of the regulars from the Smithy Bar in Dumbarton Road which, apparently, had been Sannys favourite place. As there was no service as such, the manager of the bar, an organised and affable man who introduced himself as James, offered to say a few words about Sanny before the committal, which Ella found touching, and not too long-winded or sentimental. She was surprised to learn somethings about him from the short eulogy that she had not known before. Apparently, Sannys poetry was rather good, and recitals had been appreciated by pub regulars before his recent, increasingly aggressive behaviour had got him barred from the Smithy along with some other bars around Partick.

The cafe at Kelvingrove Art Gallery was rather busy due to school holidays and tourists, so the two ladies had to wait for a table. Afterwards, they both headed out towards the bridge on Kelvin Way, and having waited for a few minutes until no one was around, Ella removed a large plastic urn from a carrier bag, and with Patsys' assistance, undid the screw top and poured the contents of ash and dust over the red sandstone parapet wall, watching the flowing milky haze as the remains of Sanny drifted down into the cloudy water of the River Kelvin.

"Aww," declared Patsy, "It looks like an angel with wings."

They paused respectfully for a few minutes as the small, animated cloud descended, and disappeared into the gently flowing water far below, then they retraced their steps to the Gallery for another cappuccino.

"People have been so sympathetic Patsy," declared Ella stirring her cup and eyeing up the meringues on the plate between them. "And I couldn't have managed without you."

Patsy leaned across the table and reassuringly touched her friend's arm.

"It's what friends are for darling."

About a month after Sannys funeral, and once her friend Ella had got the estate sorted out and had made the pleasant discovery that her widows pension was more than expected, Patsy suggested they have a day out. "Somewhere nice and classy," stated Patsy.

"Good idea, shall we meet at the Gallery?" She concluded.

When Ella arrived at Kelvingrove, Patsy was waiting, having arrived early to secure a more discreet table in the corner beside one of the massive stone pillars which supported the grand hall.

As it was quiet for a moment, Patsy organised her folder of travel and destination options for Ellas arrival.

Ella had a bright new dress, new accessories, and a fresh, calm look of confidence and empowerment.

Patsy clapped her hands to applaud Ella as she curtsied, then sat down to join her friend.

Coffee and meringues arrived, thanks to an arrangement, and small bribe to a member of staff, and the two girls looked at each other knowingly.

There was a brief, but tangible silence between them, until Ella broke the impasse with a smile and a sweeping gesture of her manicured hand out towards the gallery around them.

"I could buy one of these paintings," she declared, observing Patsy's reaction carefully.

"Of course you could, darling, . . . a small one"

There was a moments slightly awkward silence, broken by Patsy who continued, "They sell prints in the gallery shop you know, good quality ones, you can get them framed yourself along at the art shop in Hyndland Street."

Ella did not seem too impressed.

"I was at Rita Rusks the stylists yesterday," stated Ella, "Do you think they did a good job?"

Patsy squinted her eyes towards Ella's new hair style, "Yes it looks expensive darling."

Ella gazed back impassively towards her friend and then stirred her cappuccino which was now cooling. To save any further awkwardness Patsy pulled out her folder of travel options.

"We should make the most of summer now and go for a classy day out," stated Patsy, enthusiastically.

"How about a cruise in the Med," purred Ella, examining a recently purchased bracelet hanging heavy on her wrist, which matched two new rings on her fingers.

"Ohh! . . . one thing at a time darling, you know I don't like water much,"

"You never have learned to swim, have you Pats?" enquired Ella cheekily, leaning over and poking her friend in the arm.

They both laughed of the idea of Patsy trying to swim in the Med and proceeded to pour over the travel options. They agreed, the time was right for it, and no one would think it too near to the funeral.

Ella removed a list from her new handbag, placing it on the table and giving Patsy time to get ready for her big plan. They agreed, not Glasgow, it was too near. Edinburgh would be too obvious, even with the fancy restaurants and historic sites.

Also, Ella, although she would not say it directly, did not want to be an audience for a prolonged period of Patsy's artistic gushings as they walked around the Edinburgh galleries. Patsy could be such a snob!

Stirling would be too parochial, Perth, too small and cold, London, too far, and Newcastle, too busy with shoppers. York was considered for a few minutes being historic without too many galleries to distract Patsy.

"We can go to the Grand Hotel in York for an overnight girls party," suggested Patsy, but Ella was still undecided, "And how abouts it be your treat to me for supporting you over these last few months," added Patsy, giving Ella a slight shock at the suddenness of the request.

Ella stared into the echoing hall surrounding them, and after a few seconds of consideration, seemed to resolve on a reply, looking directly across the table to Patsy, "Of course it will be my treat Pats, I could not have managed without you. "But!" she swiftly added, "If I'm paying, I get to choose the venue."

Patsy agreed immediately.

Three weeks later Patsy boarded a train at Glasgows' Queen Street Station bound for Helensburgh, fifty minutes travel-time down the Clyde coast, and alighted to sunshine and a brisk on-shore breeze, which flapped and clattered the furled sails of the boats docked in the marina as she headed to meet Ella in a small coffee shop, for which Ella had given clear directions.

"It's a good thing you put on that heavy coat of yours Pats," said Ella as her friend entered the Terrace Coffee House at Colquhoun Square. "It's lovely out, but still cold for summer, and we're having a walk along the prom today to clear the cobwebs," she added, enthusiastically.

"Dinner and champagne tonight at the Rosslea Hall!"

Patsy gasped in approval, "Oh, it's so classy and discreet, and I was at such a lovely wedding there two years ago, I do hope they might remember me."

Ella froze briefly, but soon regained her composure, and smiled at Patsys bubbly enthusiasm for the venue.

The walk along the seafront was breezy, and although the distance to Rosslea Hall was several miles, such was the engagement of their conversation, that the distance, even along the narrower stretches of the Gareloch Road, were soon swallowed up.

Dinner was excellent, the second bottle of champagne soon going the same way as the first. The third being consumed more slowly, with Patsy doing most of the work.

They chatted and laughed, and time flew by.

An extra treat of a large meringue was produced unexpectedly by Ella for her friend after dessert, and it was sneaked outside to be eaten discreetly in the cool night air so as not to look like Patsy was greedy.

"Oh, what a lovely day darling, you've done us proud." gushed Patsy as they walked around the main drive.

"This way Pats. Steady as we go, I think you're a wee bit pished." chirped Ella, supporting her friend by the arm.

They made their way slowly round the back of Rosslea Hall and into the adjacent Yacht Club marina.

With Ellas guiding arm, both ladies walked along the long wooden boardwalk beside the Club leading out towards an array of moored boats glinting on the water.

They stopped at the end of the walkway, Patsy's confusion beginning to show.

"We won't be getting on a boat here darling," she slurred. "Will we?"

"No, we won't," stated Ella flatly.

There was a moments silence.

"Thank you, Pats, for all you've done for me, I have really appreciated our friendship."

Patsys confusion continued to grow, alarm suddenly surging inside her.

"Darling!", whimpered Patsy.

As Patsy hit the water, the wet and icy coldness quickly saturated her coat at the same time as the excess champagne and activating sedatives buried in the meringue de-animated her brief panic. Her struggles were sluggish and short-lived, and Ella did not leave the boardwalk until she was sure that her good friend remained submerged and that everything was peacefully silent again.

She briskly returned back to Rosslea Hall to ask at reception if anyone had seen Patsy, who was suffering from depression.

On the way, Ella deeply breathed in the cool summer night air for a few moments, smiling to herself as she thought of the good times ahead.

She felt empowered,

she felt alive again,

re-awakened.

Drama at Glenclyde.

- a story relating to why security within a distillery warehouse is sometimes not so easy when the Manager is pissing some people off.

Alister McGrigor yawned, and for about the sixth time in as many minutes, glanced down at his watch to see how the time was going.

He stared out his kitchen window at the rain as it grew heavier, suddenly becoming more constant.

It looked like it was on for the day again.

He deftly flicked out a rizla paper, and filled, then rolled, then lit, his first cigarette of the day, inhaling softly and slowly to make it last.

The first cigarette of the day was always the best one.

He looked back out the window again, as the rain continued.

Ruffling his short greyish beard, he levered himself into a ragged grey cotton boiler suit, pulling the rasping zip slowly up over his ample belly then sat down to pull on a pair of battered rigger boots, which, thanks to the steel toe caps, had saved him from foot injuries many times over the years at Glenclyde Distillers Warehouse.

Glancing back towards the window, he finished up his buttered toast and drank what was left of some lukewarm tea, and lifting a green, heavy duty hillwalkers jacket from the wall peg in the hall, headed out into the morning, and down the road to Yoker railway station.

The latest copy of 'Old Glory' magazine came out from inside his jacket pocket, and he settled into the warmth of the train carriage for the short fifteen minute commute to Bowling, reading about an ongoing Fowler road roller restoration, and the finding of another rusting hulk of a Burrell show engine found slowly rotting behind a cow shed in Somerset.

Glenclydes Warehouses stood like a row of seven identical sentries standing guard along the banks of the Clyde river. Low and metal-roofed, with squat, pebble-dash rendered, whitewashed walls and hugging the shoreline, with an infrequently used cycle track, and a disused rotting wooden jetty cushioning the place from the higher coastal tides to which the river was seasonally prone.

The early twentieth century buildings had age and character, plus a full consignment of assorted maturing casks of whisky from many distilleries, all awaiting the bottling hall up in Paisley, where they would be blended, bottled and branded as 'Glentartin', 'Royal Endorsement', 'Empire Legacy', and 'Wee Cheeky Duggy' for sale around the World.

Business was good, and the Warehouses were quickly refilled just as soon as space became available.

With the recent buyout of the old Company by the Vitaevisions Corporation, a few smaller whisky businesses were consolidated under the new 'family' brand, and elsewhere, warehouses were closing, and staff were losing their jobs.

In fairness to the decision makers at head office, it was swiftly identified that Glenclyde was the most strategic, and the cheapest unit in the operation, and as such, having reduced staffing further, and with streamlined working practices, things looked good. The recommissioned forklift had been a welcome addition, along with the barcode computer system, which cut down a lot of paperwork, however, Glenclyde had its limits of operational effectiveness, being small and inefficient with its old-fashioned dunnage buildings.

It would have to do in the meanwhile, until Vitaevisions could 'reach out' for grants, and other public monies which could be secured towards investing in a bigger, more central premises of larger industrial prefabricated steel shells, which would be convenient for stock management, and in keeping with the Companies 'commitment to sustainable excellence'.

As a caring employer, they were very proud of having a fast-track, streamlined redundancy policy that secured an 'Investor in People' status.

Mr Jeremy Bickerstaff in the role of Regional Operations Director, was responsible for Glenclyde among some other duties. An assertive, thin, hairless, cold-mannered man in his late forties he yearned for recognition and status. He was understandably ecstatic when Prince Edward was cordially invited by Vitaevisions to visit after the takeover, and publicly endorse the new ownership of Glenclyde with his royal approval. Jeremy had made sure to hire a pair of red tartan trousers from a kilt outfitters up in Glasgow, and even got to shake the royal hand and participate in a brief moment of chat about golf, before the Prince was whisked off in his Range Rover to head office for a tour of the blending suite along with an introduction to some recently acquired Chinese financiers.

Jeremy was particularly delighted that the Prince commented amusingly on his red tartan 'trews', thereby justifying the expense.

As Alister alighted the train at Bowling, the rain started to clear and some lazy rays of sunshine lit up the road sweeping down to Glenclyde, the river beyond looked grey and sluggish, then suddenly shimmered gold with the sunlit promise of a fine day.

Unlocking the main front gates, he scanned the buildings ahead of him systematically and could instantly tell that all was well. It was suggested a few months ago to Mr Bickerstaff, on one of his rare visits to the premises, that as security was rather mandatory at Glenclyde, then perhaps some guard geese would be useful, the same as the variety that Chivas had brought in a while back along the road at the Ballantine warehouses. Apparently, the Chinese geese brought added a certain credibility and character to the place, and they did their job well. His boss immediately shut down the idea suggesting that all Alister wanted was the free eggs.

All was quiet and peaceful in the cool moistness of the morning air as Alister unlocked the steel door to Warehouse One, and on entering, pulled on the power switch to illuminate the entrance.

To the immediate right was the old gaugers room, a modest, windowed boxed-off unit which acted as a staff room, and just large enough to contain lockers and a basic kitchen, along with a toilet and small shower.

Alister entered, switched on the lights, and immediately checked the answering machine for phone messages. As it was only ten minutes to eight in the morning, he expected none.

He filled the kettle and having switched it on, pulled out his 'Old Glory' and continued where he had left off.

Weezil would arrive soon, but Hamish would be at least another half-hour. Weezil had been a godsend. After the last gaffer retired, Alister was asked to stand-in till a replacement could be found, and after a short period, Hamish had appeared as Mr Bickerstaffs' choice, despite having no experience in warehousing, and having spent the last three years working in tele-sales.

Hamish was physically big, but rather weak despite his size, looking a bit like a ubiquitous contemporary folk musician with a bushy brown beard.

He had a fondness for costly ethically sourced organic clothes.

Despite an acute awareness for environmentalism and climate extinction issues, he was also rather fond of his gas-guzzling, top of the range Subaru Legacy, bought for him by his mother Sandra from out of her recent divorce settlement.

A quiet, observant woman, she had, over recent years, grown tired of the men around her focussing on her petite, shapely figure, and of their frequent passing comments, with both intended compliment and unintended insult, as if they really mattered anyway. Time was short and Sandra had purpose in life; men were not a priority. Her most recent husband has lasted three years, a long time in Sandras schedule, but the settlement of divorce was very profitable for both her and her chosen family.

It was Sandra, as Hamish's mother, and trusted office secretary to Mr Bickerstaff, who secured him employment as charge hand at Glenclyde, and to assist him in supporting his lifestyle whilst avoiding too much attention or responsibility.

His sarcasm towards his team, plus his reputation for occasionally reporting his colleagues back to the office, which his mother passed on to Mr Bickerstaff, did not sit well with Alister, but worst of all was Hamish's laziness and persistence in frequently arriving to work late, and thereafter creating reasons to finish early, a situation that Mr Bickerstaff routinely chose to ignore.

After a prolonged period of this behaviour, which was impacting cask management, Hamish was reluctantly demoted and replaced by Alister as charge hand at Glenclyde, just to secure productivity, and as Hamish continued to keep his existing salary despite demotion, he was not particularly bothered.

Alister was left to manage the place, and after initially struggling with long hours and Hamishs unhelpfulness, Weezil had appeared as a temporary helper who rapidly established himself as indispensable.

Weezil was small in stature, slim, and wiry, with a tuft of black, close cropped hair above a narrow, anxious, and slightly weathered face. He was originally from Glasgow, Drumchapel, to be specific.

His mother, on realising that the adolescent boy was getting too involved with a local gang, and therefore, the local gangs access to heroin, had packed him off down the road to Bowling to stay with his gran, and to help her look after herself so as to delay a possible nursing home confinement.

Weezil had been reluctant at first to leave his familiar territory, however, on arriving at grans bungalow, he discovered he was getting a room to himself, and that the locals seemed to accept him on his general civility, and sociable merits, and despite his raggedy looks.

His small family of pet ferrets were also accepted, as they were now confined to a garden shed out in the garden where they settled immediately. Weezils mum was glad to see the back of the rodents as they were bringing a certain odour to her flat which had been causing the neighbours to gossip.

Mr Bickerstaff had taken an instant disliking to Weezil as soon as he entered the office looking for a job. The boy was clearly the 'wrong sort', and as such, was quickly sent on his way with a job application form which would immediately be binned on its return, if it returned.

Shortly there-after however, on perusing painters quotations for re-whitewashing the warehouse walls, it occurred to Mr Bickerstaff that he could save a fortune, and thereby make his figures look good if he hired a mechanical hoist, and employed the young lad from Drumchapel to do the job. Sandra prompted the idea, suggesting that it would make for serious savings in costs.

Thereafter he could just sack the boy, and no-one would bother.

Mr Bickerstaff thought through the options for dismissal, then settled on the 'wash my car' trick where he would arrive with his Jaguar and ask the boy to valet it, having placed a twenty pound note in the boot under the golf bag. As soon as the money was 'stolen', there would be an enquiry, suspension, then dismissal.

All was going to plan, and Weezil was dutifully employed, making speedy and impressive progress with his painting job, which was all but finished in six weeks, and to a good standard.

The lad was clearly a grafter, and Alister took to him immediately, showing him round the warehouses and introducing him to the casks. Weezil asked the right questions. He showed a genuine interest, and importantly, Alister felt he now had a proper grafter who would make his own working life a lot easier.

On completion of the painting, Mr Bickerstaff arrived to inspect the results, and after a quick glance in the direction of the warehouses, gestured to Weezil to wash his Jaguar saloon, to which the lad duly complied. Thirsty minutes later, Weezil appeared at the gauger's room to announce that the Jaguar was valeted, and that he had uncovered a twenty pound note in the boot, under a set of golf clubs, and, in front of Alister, returned it to the manager who feigned appreciation on the lads integrity.

Mr Bickerstaff was not pleased, but as he had no second plan for dismissing Weezil, and as Alister insisted that he was useful, and a good worker, Weezil stayed.

The sound of a rattly old bicycle could be heard outside on the road, clattering and bouncing over the shingle adjacent to the walls of the building. Shortly thereafter, Weezil appeared, dishevelled, and his usual self, smelling slightly of the ferrets he had been feeding, watering and cuddling earlier in the morning before heading off to his work.

Tea was made and the two sat down to one of the few moments of quiet in their day.

"So, . . . ye wee muppit," Alister paused cheerily to check his pencilled list, ". . . We've that stash of casks in block three to move over to block six, then replace with that fresh lorry of deliveries arriving about two, all fresh fill bourbon, and as they're all Heaven Hills, 'cos I checked with the cooperage yesterday, we should have no trouble getting an even stack four-high with standard planks and wedges."

Weezil looked across enquiringly, "There's still the cask tapings in block four, which would be lighter work for your creaky old bones!"

Alister smiled at the cheek, and looked back at his list again, "We will get Hamish to do that, seeing as he won't be any use for rolling or stacking."

Weezil looked across knowingly, "It will take that lazy tosser the next two days to do that!" he stated.

"I know", concluded Alister, "We just have to get on with it, son".

"We can update the barcode readings in block two later on, and if we have time, maybe collect some of those two hundred samples for the blenders office."

There was the sound of an approaching car out on the roadway, travelling rather too fast, and sounding aggressive. Hamish was early today . . . so only fifteen minutes late.

As he parked his Subaru outside the door, he revved the engine a few times whilst it remained stationary, just to endorse his presence.

Oddly, this morning, the sound of two car doors closing could be heard instead of the usual one.

Alister and Weezil looked up from the gaugers room table to see an anonymous looking, and expensively suited man accompany Hamish into their Warehouse, whom Hamish had agreed, on behalf of the office, to provide with a tour of the facilities. The stranger grinned through the gauger room window and proffered a fleetingly cheery, insincere wave.

Hamish stuck his head through the door and explained that the stranger was a customer, and invited for an official tour, and that any cask taping task would have to wait till another day.

The two of them disappeared around the warehouses, and that was the last that Alister and Weezil saw of them.

The Subaru drove off about lunch time towards the Erskine bridge to meet Jeremy at Mar Hall for a business lunch, and perhaps a round of golf as well, to finish off the day.

After finishing their tea, Alister and Weezil carried on with the work, methodically moving and stacking casks with the support of the reliable, if rather dilapidated, recommissioned yellow Hyster S2.5 model forklift, a small machine, but versatile enough to do the job in and around the narrow, confined stacks of casks.

It was around four o'clock that Alister noticed that the side door of warehouse seven, the farthest away block, was laying open.

As it had been locked on his checks the previous day, Alister concluded that Hamish had included a viewing of the old casks lodged at the back of this warehouse, where the best of the best of Glenclydes whiskies were discreetly stored. Viewings in warehouse seven were rare, and not generally encouraged by management.

The next morning, Hamish phoned in sick.

He had enjoyed his task on behalf of the office of showing a new potential customer around the facilities. The client was a wine wholesaler owner in Londons west end, and as such, was worth cultivating as a contact. The afternoon golf followed by heavy drinking at the Mar Hall bar had left all three men the worse for wear, but such were the challenges and sacrifices of business hospitality.

It seemed to go well, and enthusiastic soundings were made by the client to purchase a range of casks for 'in house' bottlings at his numerous high street outlets.

He had been particularly inquisitive about the older casks in warehouse seven, and Hamish was naturally keen to tell him all he wanted to know, and he considered it only right and proper to offer the guest a few cask-drawn samples on location as an 'appetiser' towards preparing the paperwork for a sale.

Hamish enjoyed this role, waxing lyrical about the heritage, provenance, exceptional excellence, and ultra-exclusivity of the hand-picked barrels reposing untouched in their slumbering sleep of long, long, long years.

On returning to his car at the entrance, the client had asked to use the toilet in the gaugers room, and on returning to the Subaru after, commented on an audible water leak under the cistern.

It was agreed with Mr Bickerstaff, that as Hamish just happened to know a local, and cheap, plumber, that repairs would be made.

Everything was very agreeable, despite the lack of cask sales resulting from the visit.

Weezil looked perplexed, "That puddle of water in the toilet will need mopping," he stated.

"It was'na there yesterday . . . you can hear the hiss from out the pipe itself, must be a weakness in the copper."

Alister rolled another cigarette, tucked it behind his right ear, then had a look for himself at the toilet.

Right enough, a thin spray of water was misting the wall under the cistern, and upon further discussion, it was agreed that its sudden presence was bemusing to the two men, so they shut off the water valve at the mains and used buckets filled from the outside tap until repairs could be undertaken.

Alister phoned the office.

Sandra answered and casually informed them that all was in hand.

The following day a small, rather shabby, white van rolled up at Glenclyde, stating, in recently applied red plastic letters, O'FLYNN, PLUMBER, 24HOURS/HERE TO HELP.

Weezil looked suspiciously at the van, then more so at the driver, a weedy looking character with thin mousey hair and tortoiseshell plastic glasses, which, due to the amount of frame around the lenses, covered much of the wearers face masking his features. A wispy moustache and beard added to the effect, rounded off with a dark blue generic boiler suit. He introduced himself as Daire, from Ennis, in County Clare, but now living in Dumbarton.

He seemed brisk, pleasant, civil, and watchful.

Daire unloaded his van by the door and then entered carrying a grubby tool box, a roll of new green garden hose on a reel, and several lengths of twenty two millimetre copper piping which he deposited outside the gauger's office before promptly asking for a cup of tea, . . . and a biscuit too, two in fact, as they were plain biscuits with no chocolate coating.

"Hey, grandpa, have you seen him round here before?" Weezil asked the gaffer, as they headed out to warehouse three.

"No, Err, I can't say I have," retorted Alister, scratching his beard as he thought some more on where the plumber might have come from.

Weezil quickly concluded, "He will be some daftie connected with Hamish, we know what to expect with that lazy big tree-hugger!"

As expected, the stacking of the casks went as easily as planned, thanks to the trusty forklift and ease of access within warehouse three. The job was all but done by mid-afternoon so Weezil took the opportunity to start the cask tappings in warehouse four.

Alister took the opportunity for another roll-up cigarette out in the sunlight but was interrupted at one point by the plumber Daire, walking along the link path in front of the warehouses.

He stopped for some pleasantries, and reassured Alister that he was just checking for additional dormant plumbing leading from the staff room, and waving cheerily, he headed off down the line of buildings.

That was the last that Alister or Weezil saw of Daire. He departed as suddenly as he arrived.

Back at the gauger's office, the plumbers van was gone, and Alister immediately checked the toilet and found that all was in good order. A section of copper pipe had been neatly replaced.

He put on the kettle and as it began to hiss and heat, rolled himself another cigarette for the walk back to the railway station.

As the kettle finished boiling and switched itself off, Weezil appeared, still holding a three pound mallet in one hand, and a barcode scanner in the other.

"Ma' effin' arms killing me y'old dafty, so how abouts you finish the tappings tomorrow morning and give me an hour to change the oil in the forklift?" Weezil glared humorously at his boss, who scowled back to cover the grin on his face.

Alister breezed, "How about seeing as I'm the smelly old fart that keeps this ship afloat, that you just finish the job and let me finish reading my 'Old Glory'."

"You should be in that magazine!" exclaimed Weezil, "As one of the restoration projects!"

"Oooh ! Ya cheeky bizzim," laughed the older man.

"It would take a lot of gloss paint to cover your rust" retorted Weezil.

"You will be thanking me later, when you're a big boss with Vitae, after ALL the stuff and tricks of the trade that I've taught you ... you ungrateful wee nuggit."

They laughed and then finished their day at Glenclyde with mugs of tea, a biscuit, and a freshly repaired toilet cistern.

The following day was business as usual, with Alister doing the cask tappings. He used a lighter hammer, as he had a better ear for the thump as the hammer hit the barrel-ends in the stacks. A light thump meant a full cask, then as the casks became emptier, the sound of the thumps would go down in tone. The empty casks, where content had leaked or evaporated over the years, would be the deepest in tone. This was a time-tested and simple way of managing cask content and recording results on a pad along beside reference digits on the electronic bar code reader.

It was a boring job, especially where access to casks was awkward, and stacks exceeded five high.

Then a ladder would be required.

Changing the oil in the fork-lift, was, by comparison, the easy option, but Weezil did have a knack for mechanical stuff, and having changed the grade of oil used in the hydrolics, the Hyster now worked a lot better than it had used to.

Hamish cut some of the warehouse grass using the sit-on mower, so even he made himself useful.

The next day was different.

Alister, being the first to arrive, was the first to discover a police car sitting outside the locked steel gates.

A policewoman was sitting casually on the bonnet of the car and gestured Alister over to her as he approached.

After a brief interview in which it was explained that 'something had happened, but she couldn't say what', the two of them entered Glenclyde and the kettle was put on with enough water for an extra cup of tea. Weezil arrived shortly thereafter rattling slowly down the path on his bike, looking alarmed as he witnessed the policewoman sitting sipping tea in the gaugers office.

Soon, Jeremy Bickerstaff's Jaguar swept into the drive and along with the driver were his secretary Sandra, a folder in her arms, and a second police officer, a tall, youngish man, clearly taking direction from the policewoman still sitting drinking tea.

Mr Bickerstaff was trembling with rage.

After a few minutes waiting for Hamish, who never showed, the policewoman calmed down the manager a little then organised Mr Bickerstaff to lead them to warehouse seven.

The secured door was opened, and police flashlights were produced by the two officers who seemed to know exactly which end of the building to go to.

Behind a short row of three grand-looking ex-sherry butts, there was, within the narrow confined space bordering the outside brick wall, a very neatly arrayed section of copper pipe, linking, by use of self-tapping valves, all three casks near their bases on the head-end. The copper pipe was joined to a garden hosepipe which snaked out through one of the low-level air vents which were spread around the building wall for air flow. Small holes had been drilled into each of the cask bungs to allow air intake as the casks emptied of their content through the pipes.

Photographs were taken. Mr Bickerstaff remained tight-lipped and quietly trembling.

Outside, the hose wound loosely down the slope of still-uncut grass, which concealed its presence, and through the lattice wire security fence, and towards the cycle track beyond.

An early morning dog walker had been strolling along the track, a small tubby man in sports gear and with a mission to 'get fit'.

As he stooped to pick up some more dogs mess in a small purple plastic bag, he noticed the strong smell of whisky, and good stuff too, old stuff!

As a whisky drinker himself, he was much amused to find the end of a hose pipe, weaving through from under the Warehouses perimeter. At the end of it was attached a small plastic valve, now closed, with the last few, residual drops still in the pipe, and a small damp patch drying rapidly on the grass, which smelled lovely.

He emptied his thermos flask of warm green tea, shook it out, then filled it with the remaining drops of lost liquor still nesting within the hosepipe. He half-filled his flask, which was ample reward.

Thereafter, having gained fresh energy, and an exciting mission too, he jogged home to feed the dog, then phone the police.

The two police officers drew aside from the others to consult together.

They then conferred with Mr Bickerstaff, who subsequently looked even more angry.

Back at the gaugers office, forensics were called in, and Alister and Weezil were formally suspended pending disciplinary action relating to damage, theft, and excise avoidance.

Sandra would phone Hamish and let him know the situation, and what was required.

The policewoman, now established as being a sergeant, thanks to some prompting by Sandra to her boss, was polite, but firm. The site was closed pending further investigation, and all staff, including Mr Bickerstaff had to report to Dumbarton Police Station that very morning, to get fingerprints taken.

The following day, Alister and Weezil met up together at a local pub called the Bay Inn, just for a talk and some mutual reassurance.

"If I get sacked son, I think I might cope with the finances by doing a bit of gardening for the neighbours," exclaimed Alister over a pint of Guinness.

"What about prison, they only need enough on us to make it easy for them to tie things up and we could be years inside, what with the amount that's lost," fretted Weezil, staring across his tonic and lime wedge at the dart board anchored to the wall beyond.

There was a moments pensive silence, broken by Weezil thinking aloud, "It's not as if those bastards need to prove it was us, so much as us needing to prove it wasn't us."

Alister pondered the simple logic of his young helpers thoughts.

"We need a distraction son," he concluded. "Listen ya' wee scrotum, we need to be doin' something, so how 'abouts a walk along to what's left of Littlemill, just for a look?".

The two suspects left the Inn, turning right and westwards, along Dumbarton Road, soon arriving outside of the rotting shell of Littlemill distillery, a sorry place of neglect and forgetting.

Littlemill was just across the road from their place of work, but, fortunately for them, under alternative ownership, and poor custodians the owners were too. Unlike the neat and tidy Glenclyde, Littlemill had, despite having considerable historic significance, been recently shut down and was now surrounded with wire mesh fencing, topped with barbed-wire, and thereafter allowed to crumble, a situation aided by some local kids adopting the poorly-secured distillery as a den and meeting place. It smelled of piss and wet and occasional fires. Latterly, a large fire had gutted what was left of the roofs, a situation blamed on locals, but rumour had it, more to do with paid arsonists, than with the local kids.

They squeezed their way discreetly through a known small gap in the fence and explored the blackened walls inside. Alister shivered at the memories suddenly awakened. They toured the remains slowly for about an hour, kicking burnt rotting casks and patting the flaking, yellowing whitewashed walls, now grey with smoke and ash.

"I mind back when Wullie and Aleck worked this place, good lads too, but sad that the drink got to them." mused Alister, he chuckled, "It's a wonder that anything got made when they were pished half the time," he paused, reflecting, "And no wonder when dipping the liquor was half their shitty wages for the week anyway!"

Weezil suddenly interrupted, "Think about it grampa, our fingerprints won't be on any of the plumbing, except for where we checked in the toilet".

They paused, and thought some more, then leaving Littlemill, headed back to their homes, and tomorrow, as they readily agreed, would be another day.

Ms Somi Singh was highly recommended by MorganStanley Associates as an executive to Vitaevisions, as it transitioned operational interest further into scotch whisky, and as MorganStanley were significant shareholders, there was little resistance to her appointment from the board. Ms Singh was rather partial to quality liquors, and appreciated a good malt, and being very competent as well, was ideal for the job. Younger and cosmopolitan, she fitted their desired profile.

It was her task to manage the internal investigation of the recent theft of three casks worth of thirty five year old Glen Grant single malt whisky from Glenclyde. She met with Sargent Coleman at Dumbarton Police Headquarters who had been the first to attend the crime scene and was now in charge of investigations. She had enjoyed their brief liaison, which was both informative and entertaining. Sandra in Mr Bickerstaffs office was particularly helpful, much of it without any prompting or need for any soliciting questions.

Jeremy was not so helpful, being surly, dour, uncooperative and, for some reason, had taken an instant dislike to Ms Singh. She avoided using his first name when communicating.

The value of lost stock was placed at six hundred thousand pounds.

Heads would have to roll.

Hamish was arrested and interviewed, but shortly thereafter released without charge.

He resigned shortly thereafter on Sandras advice, to avoid being sacked.

Alister and Weezil received written warnings for not observing better security awareness but returned to work several days later.

Sandra was promoted to Site Team Leader at Glenclyde.

Jeremy was, after substantial internal investigation, invited to accept a package of severance, which he accepted reluctantly.

The three empty casks were removed and replaced with fresh stock.

Ms Singh was complimented by the board on a discreet, hassle-free resolution to their sudden operational issue, which fortunately did not attract any media attention.

A few weeks later, on a Saturday morning, Weezil met up with Sandra in a coffee shop in Glasgow.

Sandra had always considered it important to look after family, and her nephew was one of them.

"Thanks aunty San, for getting me the job," said Weezil, "and for helping me keep it after all the shite thats happened."

She looked across her mug of coffee knowingly, "Hamish was never cut out for it, you're more suited, and Alister likes you, you both carry the place well ...and ", continued Sandra, "I was just sick of that leering incompetent Jeremy, and weak with it too." She stared at the ceiling briefly, thoughtfully, pursing her lips. "He needed to go. Hamishs' plan worked a treat. He will do fine at that London wine place, more sitting around talking and 'ambassadoring' or whatever."

"And the whisky, where did that go then?" asked Weezil.

Sandra just smiled and made no immediate reply.

Shortly, after some reflection she responded, "Let's say it's now recovered to where it should be, and Somi and I have sorted things out satisfactorily, we can work together ...we are business people."

80

Weezil smiled, confused.

"Can Alister stay as long as he wants till he retires?" the lad asked.

"Yes, of course he can", replied Sandra, "Bosses like me value stability, and," she continued, "your new assistant starts in three weeks, and he's a good wee worker too, his names Bobby Singh"

Weezil paused, letting the news sink in.

"Can we get a new forklift?" he asked.

"No, you can't!" replied his boss.

Bobby.

- the fall and rise of a whisky drinker in the face of adversity.

Bobby McQueen looked towards the clock on the wall above the cooker, then turned his attention to his breakfast, first blowing over his hot mug of coffee before sipping slowly to check if had cooled enough to allow for a proper, refreshing gulp.

Most days started this way now that he was retired.

Bobby had been a builder all his life. The wear and tear of decades of lifting and stressing had taken its toll, forcing him, on the orders of Nessie, his loyal wife, to retire on his seventieth birthday.

Two years later he still missed the tools, the people, the banter, the bustle and the building of buildings.

A small, stocky man with a practical attitude and an outdoors complexion, he had the right build to be a builder, and a good builder too, reliable, decent, and therefore, never out of contracts, with one successful job leading to another.

He kept a book, a photo album, a large one with each page showing a different project completed over the years. It held his memories and was witness to a productive life. Bobby frequently felt the profound satisfaction of being a self-made man.

It was sort-of expected that he would not last long on retiring, as he was hardly an armchair and slippers sort of man, but it was Nessie that was the first to go. She taken suddenly by an infection, which the doctors never got round to naming despite all the consultations and pills.

Life then became a lot lonelier for Bobby.

Over the months following the funeral, he steadily became more uncomfortable alone. He had never had to fend for himself, Nessie had fussed over him, cooking meals, keeping the place tidy and being there to talk to, or to keep silent company as needed. He built their bungalow himself, on the outskirts of Callander, just by Kilmahog, a spot chosen by Nessie as she loved the nearby Trossachs. The A821, also known as the Duke's Pass, was her favourite part of Scotland.

As with every successful loving relationship, they had also become good friends, and there was little left unsaid between them over the decades.

All he had now were memories, so now he was adrift in time, and to his only daughter Jenni, it had started to show itself.

They met frequently, as often as Jenni could manage, along the road in the local town of Callander. Bobby loved the walk, first thing in the morning, while the air was still cold and refreshing. He would stroll along with his black metal walking stick and embrace the freshness of the new day as the picturesque town appeared ahead of him. There were plenty of coffee shops to choose from. Some of them were quite good, what with their fresh baked scones and such, and it was also an opportunity for some proper food, as he could not cook. Nessie had always done that.

Today's destination was a little further along the road, but well worth the effort, the Puddingstone Place Cafe. Bobby actually preferred Pip's coffee shop, but it was Jenni's choice this time, and he was always glad to see her getting on in life, especially now she had been promoted in her nursing job, and time was more precious to her than ever before.

Jenni waved cheerfully towards her dad as he shuffled in through the door with his broad walking stick in hand and beckoned him over to a welcoming seat by a small sunny window table.

The cream scone was already there, and after a few minutes deciding, Jenni also ordered soup, a roll and a couple of hot macaroni pies. Dad was not eating properly these days, and it showed.

"How's wee Oola gettin' on at school darlin'," he enquired, allowing the pies to cool a bit more before consuming them.

"Ooch! She's doin' just fine what with the wee projects on the go, now that she's finishing secondary school this term."

Bobby listened intently. Family mattered to him.

"Will I be gettin' a wee visit from her then to hear about these projects?"

"Leave it with me, Dad. I will get her to organise it soon."

There was a pause, and an audible silence between them.

Jenni lifted her cup, sipped, summed up courage, then asked, "Are you managing by yourself Dad?"

"Aw bless you pet, I'm doing fine," he paused, grinning, "after all, I always keep a bottle of malt in the kitchen, and it keeps me going, . . . so it does."

Jenni looked back, concerned, "Just the one bottle then, is it Dad?"

He laughed but chose not to reply till he had found a suitable come-back, "Aye, only one bottle at a time, hen."

Jenni looked at him accusingly, "Dad, how much are you drinking now mum's away?"

She waited impatiently, annoyed at the lack of response.

"I will really have to keep more of an eye on you Dad," she sighed, staring blankly into the middle-distance of their window table.

On the way back home, Bobby stopped by the high-street whisky shop and gazed at the bottles in the window. Prices seemed to be going up every month these days he thought, as he entered. A young man called Fanshawe with a big bushy beard and a muted tweed waistcoat grinned across the counter, "Oh, hello there, what can I get for you today Robert?" Bobby did not bother to correct the lad as to his name, after all, it did say Robert, not Bobby on the debit card which he used most times. The young man had never asked him for his real name anyway.

Bobby was feeling curious, "Tell me son, what would you recommend I buy for a change?"

The younger man gazed deliberately around the shelves either side of the shop, then settled on a wine-coloured rectangular cardboard box containing a bell-shaped bottle with a plastic stag's head stuck on the front. "Dalmore 12 years old, just excellent, so sm-o-o-o-o-th, and rich, totally Christmas cake, with suggestive chocolate fricassee and fig compote, drizzled in delicate mulled-wine spices"

Bobby looked at the bottle, then at the salesman, then back at the bottle before saying,

"Aye, all right then, I'll take it."

Back home, Bobby made a cup of tea and listened for a while to the silence crowding around him, His tea became cold and skipping his planned dinner of tinned soup and a roll, he opened the Dalmore for a dram. It was slightly less than the salesman had suggested it was, however after the fifth pour, it was started to liven up a bit, so long as he did not add any water.

It was nearly one in the morning when he spotted the clock on the mantlepiece and shuddered at the remaining half a bottle sitting by him on the table. Telly had been rubbish, as usual, but he still watched four hours of it whilst topping up his tumbler with more fills.

As he got up to switch off the T.V. he suddenly felt the wobble of an oncoming head spin.

Slowly he fell forward, looking to break his fall with the coffee table by his side.

Even as he reached for it, it tipped over beneath him, and he crashed to the floor, with his left ankle giving him a blast of pain, then numbness from the knee down. The open bottle fell to the carpet glugging most of what was left into the tightly woven patterned wool fibres.

The following morning Oola phoned her mum from her Grampa's house.

"Mum, mum, your no gonna believe this, but grampa's fallen last night and burst his ankle. I phoned for an ambulance and he's gettin' taken to Forth Valley Hospital at Larbert," she continued hurriedly, her voice rising in panic. She paused to breathe before blurting out, "He's broken his ankle and his nose, and there's an empty bottle of whisky on the carpet, and he just looks like shit, and he might die!"

Her mother hushed her to calm down, "I will come straight over now, stay where you are."

The thin and greying admissions consultant looked slowly up from a medical folder, already turning fat with preliminary scans, printouts, unfilled forms, and paramedic reports.

He sighed quietly in Bobby's direction. "You have an inflamed talocrural joint Mister McQueen, but the x-ray shows no sign of breakage. You can leave later today, but someone will need to help you at home and", he concluded, "you had probably best to stay off the drink for a while, especially with the painkillers I am prescribing for you."

The medical man looked back at his patient notes, "Oh . . . and your family are here, so I suppose you will want to see them. . . will I send them in?"

Jenni and Oola swept into the emergency cubicle, in which Bobby lay obediently on an wheeled trolley.

"Dad, now listen! Were you pished last night? Is that the reason you fell?" Jenni demanded.

Oona started to cry.

"No!" protested Bobby, indignantly.

"Well then Dad," stated Jenni grimly, "we just went by the house, and saw an empty bottle of Dalmore laying on its side on the carpet."

Bobby tried to interrupt, but Jenni would not be stopped, "And," she continued,

"I saw the receipt in the kitchen, and it was only bought yesterday, so you drank THE WHOLE BOTTLE, Dad, ALL OF IT, and it wasn't even shared."

"But darlin'" he explained, trying to dissipate the rising tension, "most was spilled on the carpet when I fell while switching off the T.V."

Jenni paused, reflecting, frowning.

The ruse worked.

"I only had three wee shots sweetheart."

As Jenni looked away in exasperation, Oola swiftly provided a distraction.

"How are we going to get you home grampa?"

"Well, I'm working soon, so I need to get off quick." stated Jenni.

"I will go back with grampa in a taxi, and fix him a meal," suggested Oola.

This was agreed to be a good solution, and it helped to calm things down. On the way back across to Callander, grandfather and granddaughter had a good long chat, the sort that was impossible to have with his daughter. It was a lonely house without Nessie, and it was Oola's suggestion that moving temporarily to sheltered housing could be a solution. Just to see how it went.

Somewhere near Callander, which he knew and liked.

Bobby mulled it over, and thought about the costs and upheaval, but it was decided within the week that Bobby would try a month in sheltered accommodation, just a single room and kitchen apartment situated outside of town, within the grounds of Bracklinn House, a residential care facility near to Keltie Bridge.

Bobby was unsure, but as Jennie was persuasive, and Oola had instigated the idea, he agreed to it, and two weeks later, he moved a few of his possessions, familiar, meaningful items, into the small, but recently repainted lodgings. It was small, basic, and cosy.

Jenni suggested renting out the vacant house to lodgers for a month so as to ensure it was occupied, and the rent money could go towards paying for Bobby's temporary home, with what was left going towards Oola's university education, if she could get admission.

As he settled into the new location, taking his time to get used to it, Bobby told himself that it was all probably for the best. Oola made more regular visits with her mum, so seeing a bit more of the family was comforting.

Jenni surveyed his apartment approvingly on one of her first visits, which she used to discuss the lawyers, a will, and 'power of attorney' for herself.

"It's lovely here Dad," she enthused, "Nice, quiet and relaxing, with the lovely garden outside and company if you want it up at the fancy house. You're invited for afternoon tea by Matron, so it saves all these visits to coffee shops in town."

Bobby was not impressed.

"This is temporary now," he insisted, "I'm not staying here till I die! And well seeing as how the cemetery is just along the road there!" he added sarcastically, "Everything well on hand for my needs, except the whisky shop. Will you bring me a wee bottle of malt on your next visit darlin?" he asked

"Sure Dad" replied his daughter, making a mental note to passively forget his request.

Two weeks later, and after several rather boring attempts at afternoon tea up at Bracklinn House, Bobby found himself spending more and more time alone in his new apartment. It was nice, nothing to complain about, but something had changed, and at times he yearned to be back at his old home at Kilmahog. He appreciated the visits and chats with his new temporary housekeeper, a local lady called Kate, with a breezy disposition, and a ready laugh, however, he thought often that it would be good to get back to the *normal* of the old-days.

Jenni phoned, "Dad, good news, just fantastic, Oola's delighted too.
. . . I finally got my promotion at Stirling Community Hospital as resources manager, so, no more nursing for me now, and the pays so much better now I'm in admin too."

She paused, awaiting the applause from her father. "I don't think I can visit as often, what with all my responsibilities, but Oola will see you as she's not off to uni' yet, . . . not till September."

Oola arrived at the apartment the following afternoon, in time for a brew-up and biscuits, and bristling with the excitement.

"Isn't it great news Grampa, Mum getting promotion AND a big pay rise now that she's no longer nursing, but managing."

Bobby nodded his appreciation for Jenni's success to his granddaughter. He knew it meant a lot to her and her mum. A stepping-stone to better things in life, and more opportunities, especially for Jenni, leaving behind the split shifts, long hours, and lack of thanks by the public as a stressed and under-valued nurse . . . it would certainly have its benefits for her well-being.

Oola sipped her tea noisily, trying to challenge the silence within her Grampa's apartment.

Bobby stirred his mug, thought to himself briefly, then looked gently towards the young woman sitting across from him, "Your mum says that the rent from my house will be going towards your costs at university," he paused, awaiting a response. Oola looked awkward and a little guilty.

"So, I really need to stay here now, so you and your mother can get on with it."

Oola looked nervously away towards her cup, "Sorry . . . Mum's decided, she feels it's for the best."

Bobby felt tears well up behind his eyes but kept the emotion silent and inside of himself.

"Well that's fine then." he concluded, as if surprised at his easy acceptance of the new reality.

Oola, sensing something serious, blurted, "But they're very nice people in your house Grampa, keeping it lovely, clean and tidy," she paused, "so Granma would be pleased!"

Bobby smiled to himself, and finally broke the long silence that had settled between them between them by saying "Well that's sorted then. I stay here, your mum gets an easier job, and you, my sweetheart, go off the uni, and out into the big bad world." He paused again, "Well!" he sighed, "We all better just get on with it I suppose, . . . what is it your studying for anyway?, . . . will there be a job at the end of it?"

Oola looked up, "Social sciences, it's what I really want to do, environmental planning"

Bobby nodded, then poured them both some more tea out of the pot.

"There's just one thing mind, so that I will agree to it all, what with me stuck here now," he leant towards his granddaughter, lowering his voice into a conspiratorial, but loud whisper, "I want you to deliver me whisky when I need it. About two bottles a week will be enough, I will give you the money."

Oola nodded in agreement to the proposal, grateful to be past the awkward bit.

Oola never bought him any whisky. . . she forgot and eventually spent the money he gave her on clothes for herself.

Initially, Bobby made it successfully along the main road to Callander and into a coffee shop, usually Pip's, then afterwards, onto the whisky shop for a couple of bottles. Single malts, of course.

Soon though, the weight of the bottles began to get heavier as he returned along the road towards his apartment, and it did not help either that staff at Bracklinn House were now whispering.

His home help brushed off the tittle-tattle of rumour and gossip broadcast from the House as she clearly saw that he paced his drinking, and that no signs of binging were evident in his manner or behaviour towards herself and others. For a while, her gravity and sensibility prevailed successfully in protecting Bobby from darker forces, but this was not to last.

Jenni visited a few times, but less and less often than before, thanks to the demands of her admin job, which was proving more stressful than expected. The tablets proscribed to her helped, but they made her concern for the out-side world and her family less acute. On hearing from management at Bracklinn House that her father was drinking too much, and probably posed a risk to himself and the apartment, she made a special point of phoning.

"Dad, now listen," she intoned, "You need to cut down on the whisky. Oola and I are very, very worried, and it's not fair on the care team at Bracklinn who are so very worried about you too". There was a brief pause then, "I've been thinking that you will need more care, even though it will cost me more, I've thought long and hard about it and could never forgive myself if something happened!"

"Like what exactly?" prompted Bobby.

Jenni sighed down the phone in exasperation, concluding her call with swift mutterings of love and blessings.

Later that day, Bobby sat alone in his apartment having a few wee drams to clear his head and mellow his mood after Jenni's unsettling phone call. After a while he arose from the armchair, struggling a little to escape its cushioning embrace, switched off the telly, which was rubbish anyway, and headed out the door into the calming breeze of a quiet summer's evening. Bobby stood breathing in the cool soft air, listening to the birdsong, and watching as the vivid sunlight, cast its dramatic illumination over the passing clouds turning the blue sky, orange.

Bobby looked out into the middle distance of his mind, memories flickering and then passing to be replaced with a growing nostalgia for yesterday and before, of his work, his wife, his family, all passing by and fading softly in the presence of relentless time.

How cruel time was, to steal life so fast.

He sipped again from the tumbler in his hand, experiencing the bite of alcohol followed by the ceremony of flavours arriving with it, empowering his moment, his thoughts, his living.

Perhaps it was the whisky.

He glanced down at the glass in his hand, raising it slightly towards the sun sinking now, down over the hills beyond, he looked through the amber within the glass and saw the amber in the sky beyond.

Gradually, over the passing minutes, Bobby sensed his position in life more clearly.

Older, weaker, resigned to the rolling wheels of fate as he shuffled through the winter of his years.

He should have learned to cope at home in Kilmahog, learned to not be dependent on Nessie, or the family, not to have spent as many hours at his work, but it was too late now.

At least he still had his whisky, a lifelong companion who always sympathised with him whatever his mood, . . . always such good company.

The following morning, there was a sharp, business-like rattle on the door, which Bobby opened to reveal a small, stout, overly made-up woman, clad in the Bracklinn House uniform.

"Mr McQueen, may I come in for a chat!" demanded the woman.

Bobby stood back from the doorway and beckoned her in with a wave of his walking stick.

"That's quite a weapon you've got there Mr McQueen, we don't usually see such big solid walking sticks at Bracklinn!" she declared.

"Now, look", declared the woman, briskly viewing her file of resident notes, looking for some information, "Robert. . . right, it's Robert? Good. Now then, let's see shall we, what do we need to know and check."

Bobby felt a chill up the back of his neck but remained silent to allow more of the stranger to reveal itself.

The woman looked across the room, having found his name in the records, and now feeling organised to proceed with the purpose of her visit.

She smiled, which served to accentuate her theatrical falseness.

Sensing his wariness, she paused, moderating to a more soothing, comforting style of engagement.

"I'm such a silly!" she declared, rolling her eyes upwards, "I've not even introduced myself Robert, I'm your new carer. My name's Shona Shine, but feel free to call me Shoney, because everybody at Bracklinn does," she paused, gauging his reaction, "And we are delighted to be welcoming you up to the house next week as one of our residents."

Bobby froze, "But I'm happy here Ms Shine."

Clinging to his walking stick as dizziness gripped him, he continued before Ms Shine could repossess their conversation, "Phone Jenni, she's my daughter, she organised this sheltered apartment, and it's just fine for me, really, there's no need for me to be going up to the nursing home."

"Bracklinn House," interrupted Ms Shine, "Is NOT a nursing home as such, it's a residential community of friends and family, where everybody can be reassured of being part of a REAL home environment, and you, Robert, are now the newest member of our family, and we will be welcoming you next week with a special party organised by all your new friends."

Bobby could see the way she played with the words she used. He could sense Ms Shines' contempt.

Having said her piece, she started to leave before adding, "Jenni and I are in complete agreement that this is for the best, what with your unresolved drinking problem. After all, your welfare is our concern."

She smiled again, pausing to observe Bobby's reaction, then with a sort of sympathetic sigh, lifted a framed photo from the mantlepiece and scrutinised it closely, squinting at the loving couple.

"That must be you and Annette then, Robert?" she enquired breezily.

Bobby nodded, observing his unwelcome visitor, "Yes, that's myself and Nessie," he confirmed.

"Well, if you won't quit alcohol for your own sake, do it for her!" concluded Ms Shine. Replacing the picture, she made for the door, pulled it firmly shut behind her before making her way out onto the driveway and waddling uncomfortably back up the road to Bracklinn House.

He was in trouble, he could sense it, but experience told him he needed to give it time.

Aware of his growing anger at what had just happened, he put on his coat and grabbing his walking stick, headed outside and down the road into Callendar to buy a couple of bottles of malt.

The walk there was quite easy, the anger spurring him on, but the weight of the Springbank and Ardbeg bottles in a carrier bag made progress back to the apartment a slow business, and Bobby found himself having to sit down, and rest on a wall by the side of the road.

There was the sudden toot of car horn, no…it was a van horn Bobby realised, as he came out of his own thoughts to see an old familiar face grinning at him from the driver's seat.

The van indicator flashed on and the van stopped in a lay-by just a few hundred metres down the road.

A youngish, sandy-haired, lean man in a boiler suit jumped out, and started walking back up the road towards Bobby with the grin still on his face and his hands in his pockets.

Bobby remained seated, resting on the wall, his eyes lighting up as he recognised his old apprentice, Billy.

"Hey, Bobby, ye old rascal," shouted Billy as he approached, "I hav'ne seen you around for about two years now. How's the retirement going."

Bobby told his story, Billy listened as he perched on the wall next to his old Gaffer, it did not take long

"There can be nothing more hurtful than the good intentions of family," concluded Billy as he helped the older man into the van and drove him the short journey back to the apartment.

They had a short, but very meaningful conversation during the journey, and as Bobby got out the van, Billy said, "You can expect a visit up there at the house from me before too long old 'fella. Oh! and don't forget your bottles Bobby, fine stuff by the looks of it."

The following week, Bobby left his apartment for the last time and taking his suitcase, the framed photo, and the few ornaments from the mantlepiece, was driven the few hundred yards up to the main building in the Bracklinn House Mobility Bus. He was eventually to be ushered into a small, sparse room somewhere at the back of the large, once opulent house, a converted Victorian country retreat, originally a rich man's folly, now making money as a dumping ground for the unwanted elderly.

But first, there was to be a 'ceremony'.

Ms Shine was the first of several members of staff to welcome him in through the front door.

"Robert," she gushed, smiling and overly sincere for the benefit of those around her.

She wrapped an arm around his shoulders, embracing him even as he shuddered.

"All the girls and boys are delighted to welcome you, it must have been so lonely down in that apartment, but it has been a good middle-place for you to have before coming to join us, so you can appreciate your new community all the more."

Bobby nodded acknowledgement.

People clapped,

then wandered off.

His room was small, plain, functional, a single bed, a table and small wardrobe. Fortunately, it had one redeeming feature, a good view out the ground floor window over the manicured grass and into the rhododendron bushes beyond, littering as they were, jungle-like around the grounds, a green walled barrier against the world beyond.

Ms Shine carried Bobby's small suitcase into the room, depositing it on the bed, then lifted a bundle of printed paper from the bedside table.

"These are the rules and regulations Robert!" she stated, suddenly brisk now that there was no audience to impress.

"Read them for yourself so as you don't forget our house rules, and never think you don't have to ask me. . . if you find you forget."

Bobby smiled at the absurdity of his new world.

"Oh, and one more thing," declared Ms Shine, "No Alcohol Allowed!"

Bobby sat alone in his new room, feeling the sudden shock of change, and a growing sensation of anger.

As the night fell, and Bobby was sure he was free of further interruptions, he felt safe enough to lift out the two bottles of malt from his case. Opening one carefully, he poured a drop into his plastic bedside tumbler, sipped slowly and carefully, savouring the freedom it provided.

Shona Shine could simply not figure it out.

Where was the wee bamstick hiding his liquor!

She was an experienced professional carer and knew all the tricks in the book when it came to resident shenanigans, however, there was something about Robert McQueen that she could not figure out.

Where, oh where, was he hiding his bottles of whisky.

"Never mind", she thought to herself, "He will soon run out."

Bobby stayed in his new room for most of the day.

Jenni phoned to see that he was settling in and they spoke for all of a minute before she had to end the call due to a strategy meeting in her office.

Some mail also arrived from Oola, addressed to him at Bracklinn House, with a small crown and smiley face penned beside the address.

Oola let her grandfather know that she had a boyfriend now, called Vyshon, who was so sweet, and also that she was now off for six months with Vyshon to Perth, Australia, staying at a climate rebellion retreat to learn to share energy, and that on her return to Scotland, she would be studying Art History for four years at St Andrew's University. She added that she hoped he was keeping well and that she had been told that Bracklinn House was a lovely, caring place, and could he send her money, about a thousand pounds would do for the moment.

Bobby carefully folded the letter, tears now visible, which he brushed away quickly, and he entered his bathroom, removing the toilet cistern cover, and lifted out the last of his now wet bottle of Ardbeg.

"Ohhh! You naughty boy Robert," spat Ms Shine, pretending it was funny.

"I can smell that nasty smoky whisky of yours, even though I can't see where you hid the bottle."

"I have spoken to our Doctor," she continued smugly, "And, I will be replacing your alcohol habit with some proper medication."

"That's fine, Ms Shine!" replied Bobby.

"Oooh stop it now, you wee rascal," clucked Shona, "Really, just call me Shoney, because your part of the family now."

Bobby said nothing.

"Now I know you've got another bottle somewhere Robert, and I will find it before you finish it too, mark my words Mister."

Despite another thorough search of the room, which due to its sparsity was easy to search, Ms Shine could find no other bottle of whisky.

She was both mystified, and angry, so went off to the kitchen to launch an investigation into employee theft, due to there being white bread missing from the fridge, which she believed was being used to make toast by members of staff, and not used for residents.

Theft was theft, and disciplinary action would follow.

The next day Billy drove up in the van to visit his old friend.

Ms Shine sent a member of her team out to remind the visitor that tradesmen should park their vehicles at the rear of the building, to which Billy grinned and complied.

The two men spent several hours alone in deep discussion.

Ms Shine took some tea into the room for the two men, which was not her usual job, but it gave her the opportunity to earwig in on their conversation. They were discussing attic conversions and how to work a compact low-beam torch which Billy had brought as a present.

She left disappointed.

That night at nine p.m., after all residents were sedated and settled in bed, and the nightshift man had arrived on duty, a van drove quietly in through the front gates of Bracklinn House.

An elderly man with a walking stick, a suitcase containing, among other things, a bottle of whisky, and holding a glowing torch, emerged from the bushes and entered the van, which then drove off just as quietly as it had arrived, back onto the road, and off towards Callendar.

The following morning, Ms Shine, in a state of considerable distress, called the police on finding a resident's room window wide open, and the resident along with their possessions, missing.

"Dad," barked Jenni down the phone. "Where are you and what have you done?"

Bobby sighed and braced himself.

"Listen darlin', things have changed! Now listen carefully", he continued before Jenni could interrupt, "I don't want to take up too much of your very precious time. I'm staying at an old friend's house, never mind where, and I will not be going back to *that* place you sent me to."

"Shoney is worried sick Dad, and I think you owe her an explanation," insisted his daughter.

"Ms Shine can go fuck herself!" Bobby replied flatly. "Now you just listen to me Jenni… it's my turn now, so shut up for a bit. I am selling my old house, the people renting can buy it, if they wish. I have now moved in with some friends that I know I can trust and who can use the rent I will be paying them. If you want to meet, we can see each other at Pip's in Callendar."

"But!" retorted Jenni, "I have legal Power of Attorney over you Dad, and it's for your own best interest and safety. I will have to notify the police to apprehend you and bring you back."

"No, you won't darlin'. I never got round to signing the document, so what you have is not legal"

Jenni went silent, "Listen Dad, we can discuss this later, I have a very important meeting now and I can't talk about this anymore."

"There's nothing more to talk about. Bye, bye!" replied Bobby.

Billy grinned across the garage where to two men had been sorting out a new lock for the flat next door which had been home, until recently, to his wife's aunt.

"We can soon redecorate Bobby," chipped Billy, "But in the meantime, while my missus collects the kids from school, how abouts we celebrate your moving-in."

Billy went to collect two tumblers from the kitchen whilst Bobby pulled an unopened bottle of Springbank twelve year old from his case.

In the moments silence, Bobby looked towards the westering sun and felt its warmth on his face.

It had been a challenge, but now he felt the glow of victory growing inside him.

The whisky Billy and he shared was delicious.

Nessie, he was quite sure, would have been proud of him.

Voyage of the 'Kelpie'

- a windswept coastal tale of adversity, initiative, resolve, endeavour and conclusion.

1955 was an eventful year in the life of the M.V. 'Kelpie', a Clyde puffer of repute and character.

Captain Norrie Nimmo, master of the puffer boat 'Kelpie' was having a bad day.

Late summer rain fell cold and hostile onto Glasgow streets below as he walked into the offices on Bath Street of the long-established, and reputable, Clyde & Isles Steam Shipping Company Limited.

He felt the weight of the heavy oak front doors resist his efforts to enter the building, however, after pausing, frowning, and in deep thought, he pushed a little harder to make way to his appointment with the boss, although he had momentarily wished that the doors would have just stayed closed, leaving him out in the rain.

A bright and bustling secretary met his reluctant gaze from behind her desk as he entered the offices of Mr Nicholson, the Director and co-owner of the Company. Her positivity from behind a tastefully manicured appearance showed no sign of judgement of his plight.

The captain was asked to take a solitary seat strategically located by the door to the boss's office, where he sat quietly and alert, a small white-haired, weather-beaten, wiry, wrinkled, man with soft grey eyes and although now in his early seventies, still sprightly, and with the convincing disposition of an experienced seafarer.

As he sat nervously, impatiently contemplating the punishment for his recent mistake, his right hand reaching instinctively towards the inside pocket of his heavy wool jacket to where an unsealed letter of resignation had been penned only a few hours ago at the railway station ticket office in Port Glasgow.

Norrie was so far into his thoughts that he barely heard the phone on the secretary's desk ringing to convey the short instruction for Captain Nimmo to go into the boss's office.

He knocked briefly on the door before awaiting approval to enter, pausing to judge the right level of sound his knock would create, so, not too soft, that it might not be heard, and not too loud, that it appear to be cheeky.

"Come on in Norman," commanded Mr Nicholson from behind a large, opulent, dark wood table, which stood framed by the large picture window behind the affable, neatly dressed manager, and cast a soft natural light into the discreetly wood-panelled office, adding an extra note of authority to the man himself.

"Now just have a wee seat Captain and let's discuss the incident last week with the 'Kelpie'".

Mr Nicholson looked down at the recently opened folder in front of him containing an assortment of reports and witness statements.

Captain Norrie remained stoically impassive, keeping eye contact when needed, and looking shameful when appropriate.

Mr Nicholson let the silence grow around the two men for a minute, before proceeding.

"So Captain, let me get this right, and feel free to intervene if the facts are adrift, but on the first of September, the 'Kelpie' proceeded with normal crew to deliver fifteen tons of coal from Port Glasgow to Islay, Port Ellen to be precise, and when you had not arrived at the allotted time, the situation was not in fact reported by the Island as one might have expected" he paused. Looking across the table for a reaction.

There was none, so he proceeded, "The first known whereabouts of the 'Kelpie' was reported five hours later by the harbour master at Port Rush in Ireland, who, it would appear, found the situation highly entertaining."

Mr Nicholson paused again, placing a hand towards his brow as if registering further disbelief, he continued, "Having consumed drink at the Harbour Bar for over an hour, where crew members broadcast the mistake to all and sundry, you proceeded to exchange two bags of coal for a bottle of Bushmills Whiskey, thereafter, declaring that as there was no shortage of fuel, Islay would get their delivery anyway, and if the coal tonnage was short, they could always cut a bit more peat."

He continued, "Thereafter, the 'Kelpie' proceeded at full speed from Ireland to Islay, having disabled the ship's engine governor to do so. This resulted in over stressing the engine, which thereafter blew a boiler gasket in the Sound Of Jura, causing you to request assistance of a tow from a passing fishing trawler into Port Ellen harbour, where you gave away over a ton of coal to the trawler crew to prevent solicitation of salvage claims". Mr Nicholson pressed his lips together for a moment before continuing the recitation, "Payment from our client on Islay was promptly made for eighty percent of the cargo, the other twenty percent being presumed, either swapped for whiskey, paid as salvage hush, or burnt in the ships own boiler." He leant back in his chair as though exhausted by what he had read.

"Captain Nimmo…do you have anything to say in your defence of this shambles?"

"No, not really, it's. . . er, well. . . er, just as you said Mr Nicholson, sir," responded the Captain, staring blankly at the table in front of him.

Mr Nicholson sighed, bringing out a large manilla envelope from a pile of documents beside him, and laying it, still sealed onto the table in front of him.

Captain Nimmo went to reach to his inside pocket for the resignation letter before his boss had the chance to sack him.

He paused, as the man across the desk looked up, smiling.

"You know Norman, the worst of it is the Cal Mac officers laughing across the bar at the golf club."

He grinned. Captain Nimmo removed his hand slowly away from the resignation letter.

"Seriously Norman," he chuckled, "What the hell took you to Port Rush?"

"Well!" responded the Captain, "The manifest got dropped in the boiler room when it fell out ma' pocket, and the destination got smudged with oil. And then," he continued, "Well I just had it in ma' head we were bound for Port Rush. So, there you are then sir." he concluded, "Will you be needing my resignation Mr Nicholson?"

Mr Nicholson winked across the table, "Not today Norman, I think under the circumstances, and after forty years of service to 'Clyde and Isles', and despite you probably giving some thought to retirement, we have another wee mission for you before we think about calling it a day with the 'Kelpie'."

Norrie sighed, and relaxed a little in his seat.

"Here's your instruction Captain," said the manager, handing across the manilla envelope containing a manifest to his old acquaintance, "Proceed back down to Port Glasgow where they're finishing repairs to the engine and boiler, then, along with your new member of crew, because I know your still a man down, proceed with a mixed cargo, all crated, to Dunoon. Then to Port Bannatyne, thereafter to Tighnabruaich, then onto Crinan, your old stomping ground, for a freight of furniture for Scalasaig on Colonsay. On your return, deliver a hundred empty whisky casks currently at Bunnahabhain, across to Craighouse on Jura, before returning straight across to Loch Stornoway, where I would appreciate it if you beach the puffer on the sand for visitors at our house just up the road, to see," concluded Mr Nicholson.

Captain Norrie looked confused, "Why would anyone want to see an old puffer?" he asked.

"It's my daughter's wedding reception weekend, and guests have asked to see a puffer sitting on the sand at high tide, apparently they saw it in a movie recently and think it would be charming."

The Captain, now with the spring back in his step, hopped off the train in Port Glasgow to a brief break in the relentless rainfall, and with still threatening, rain-soaked clouds above him, walked the mile or so down to Kingston Dock.

As he approached the waterfront, the familiar sight of the 'Kelpie' appeared.

Laying eighty two foot long with a sturdy water tube vertical boiler at her heart, she had character and always seemed to draw a smile from the public, especially the children, and especially when the Captain sounded her steam horn, which he did when children were watching the boat and waving their hands for attention.

As the tide was high, it was only a broad step onto the vessel where the old Captain was greeted by his second in command, the first mate, Hingus.

Hingus Hogg looked like an undertaker, which was appropriate as he was not what one would call a cheerful man, in fact, he was dour and sullen, and felt that time aboard the 'Kelpie' was wasted time. But as he had a family to keep, and as the ship did give him the title of First Mate for his testimonial, he felt it was worth the commitment in the short term.

It did however, make him smile that, with the recent misfortune, Captain Nimmo had finally put his hands in his pockets and paid for needed repairs to the boat. Aside from a replacement gasket, the upper exterior paintwork had been refreshed to hide the more visible rust.

The Captain was not pleased to see Hingus.

"Are all the jobs I left you with done yet Mr Hogg?" he enquired in his softly spoken way.

"No." replied his second in command, "Most but not all, as command jobs are not my responsibility Captain, but yours! I have helped Mr McGhee to install the replacement gasket in the boiler, and he has now tested the governor and the engine under steam. On completing that, we have painted the rusty bits that the eye can see, but I am not painting below decks, even though you got the paint for free from your pals on Islay, and anything in the steering room is your affair Captain, and nobody else's."

The Captain paused to roll a cigarette, lighting it slowly, then inhaling deeply, keeping his number two waiting impatiently for a response.

"Well then," he murmured, knowing what Mr Hogg was waiting to hear, "No doubt you will be delighted to hear that I have found it unnecessary to resign my commission, and in fact," he drew the folded unsealed brown envelope from his coat pocket, "We will be sailing on the ebb this evening as we have some company business to attend to. I'm afraid that I have to tell you Mr Hogg that your still only second in command." With that he headed off to the wheelhouse to finish his smoke.

Hingus muttered some curses and kicked a metal bucket across the decks before heading down the foc'sle for a cup of tea with the engineer, Mr McGhee.

Beanie McGhee knew the boilers of a puffer inside out, after all, he had worked around small ships engines all his life, almost as long as he had known Norrie Nimmo, which was many decades now as they had grown up together in Oban.

Beanie was a few years younger, and of different appearance and character, being generous of nature, and of waistline too. Small, sandy haired and quick to spend his money, though not frivolously, it was not unusual that, due to the Captain's meanness with cash, he would spend his own wages on needed parts for the 'Kelpie', simply to keep her afloat.

"Here now, here now," quipped the engineer, " . . . That's awfy good o' you Hingus to make me a fresh brew, and thanks for all your help today, I could'na have managed without you, and by the way, now the Captains back aboard, where's that new member of crew we were told on Islay that we were getting?"

"No idea!" replied the first mate, "You know that the Captain tells me nothing," he whined.

"No wonder son," returned the engineer, "What with all the cheek you give him, I'm surprised he don't throw you off the boat." The First Mate looked grim but said nothing.

Later that afternoon, as the sun started to settle towards the western ridges skirting Loch Long, the 'Kelpie' slipped her moorings to collect the cargo sitting down river at Port Glasgow Docks.

Loading was completed within the hour, thanks to the energy of both Hingus and Mr McGhee, who were busy on the foredeck winch, balancing out the hold neatly with the assorted cargo, so it was the Captain, smoking in the wheelhouse who first spotted the small boy, sitting on a little, battered leather case on the dockside staring balefully at the proceedings.

Captain Nimmo sounded the Kelpies steam horn briefly and waved at the lad, who stared sullenly back.

Captain Nimmo, registering the passivity of the lad, leaned out the port-side window and shouted for him to go home. "You've heard the whistle now laddie, so you can head off home for your tea, then play with your pals, why don't you!" he exclaimed.

The young boy continued to sit impassively on the dock, until Mr McGhee had the foresight to leave the derrick in the hands of Hingus and go to investigate the odd behaviour of the watcher.

"This is the Captain lad, Captain Nimmo, and that's Mr Hogg, the First Mate," stated the engineer kindly to the nervous boy who he had just assisted aboard the boat.

"Now Mr McGhee, we have no time for sight-seeing tours of the puffer!" shouted the Captain, leaning out from inside the wheelhouse window, waving the visitor back ashore.

"But Captain, the wee lad's our new member of crew," shouted back the engineer, somewhat baffled.

Mr Hogg was commanded to take the wheel for the first hour as the puffer chuffed slowly out into the river Clyde, making westwards, down towards the Kyles Of Bute.

This gave the Captain and engineer plenty of time to quiz the newest member of the crew.

Captain Nimmo stood back, and rolled a cigarette, letting his engineer ask the questions, as Mr McGhee's manner was a little more sympathetic.

They headed down into the foc'sle for the interview.

"So," he started, having handed the lad a large tin mug of sweet hot fresh-brewed tea and a biscuit, "What's your name son and where are you from, . . . and how did you end up here?"

The young boy stared into his tea, clasping the mug in both hands as if looking for some extra warmth.

"My names Edward Gunn," he replied, "From Greenock, and my mum cleans at the offices of the Company and needed to get rid of me 'cos I've left school now."

"And what age are you then son," asked the engineer kindly."

"Twelve," replied Edward.

"Looks more like a nine-year-old tae me," huffed the Captain.

Mr McGhee cast the Captain a withering look, then returned his attention to the boy.

"Welcome aboard the 'Kelpie' sonny, and we will start your training by getting you to make us some dinner."

He gestured to the small range in the corner of the foc'sle, and having procured the eggs, bacon and potatoes from an old tea chest, proceeded to show the lad how to cook enough, but not too much, for four . . . well, three and a half.

Although Edward had burst the yolks of the eggs in the frying pan, it was agreed by all, even the Captain, that dinner had been tasty, and nicely seasoned, . . . but the tea had been watery.

That evening the 'Kelpie' drew into Port Bannatyne for the night, having made the first delivery to Dunoon without any issues or dramas. Even the First Mate was being less grumpy, had smiled a bit and shared some tame jokes with the boy.

"Tomorrow morning," stated the Captain, ". . . At first light, we make way round the Kyles, Edward, and I will show in the wheelhouse how we steer a puffer through the Burnt Islands just by Colintraive".

"So you can learn how it's not done sonny!" sneered the First Mate.

Captain Nimmo cast a scathing look at his number two but remained silent.

Mr McGhee hastily suggested a game of cards, to show the lad how poker was played.

The following morning Edward stood alone on the deck of the 'Kelpie' breathing fresh air for the first time in his short life, and suddenly feeling the awareness of a bigger, more beautiful world beyond the confines of his mothers Greenock flat. He listened to the sigh of the lapping water, and the call of the marine birds swooping low around the boat and felt a little less nervous.

His moment was not to last for long, as the First Mate arrived up on deck with a galvanised bucket and a large scrubbing brush in his hands.

"Firstly, Edward, you've to scrub the forward deck up to the life boat, then when thats done, I will gi' ye a tin of paint and a wee brush for touching up the rusty bits around the deck, and be sure and not miss any, 'cos the Captain will be checking . . . eventually!"

Navigating the Kyles Of Bute was a task for the brave and skilled.

With Edward up in the wheelhouse watching the Captain coaxing the wheel, the boat only hit some rocks once, which the Captain blamed on a strong current flowing out of the Ruel river to the north.

Mr Hogg sniffed his opinion, "Aye there, Captain, nearly made it without a scratch, but not quite."

The Captain ignored his comment and, now heading south down the Wester Kyles, let Edward have his first shot of the steering wheel, but not for too long.

Tighnabruaich sparkled in the sunlight borne on a lightness of the mornings breeze.

"Is this the tropicals?" asked Edward, pointing at the cluster of palm trees fringed around the bay of characterful houses meandering their way up and into the hills behind.

The crew laughed, "Aye lad, for about one day every year," replied Mr McGhee.

"Tighnabruaich," stated the Captain, "Is Gaelic for 'houses on a hill', so there's me getting you bilingual already."

He winked at Edward, then turned his attention to supervising the cargo discharge, ticking off the few parcelled items as they left the boats hold, to be landed on the quayside beyond.

Turning west then north by Ardlamont Point, the 'Kelpie' steamed her way steadily on calm waters and under fluffy clouds, which scattered themselves like cotton across the blue above.

Travelling up Loch Fyne towards Ardrishaig, and towards the entrance lock into the tranquil canal, by the time they reached Crinan, Edward, despite his diminutive size, was rapidly became expert at manoeuvring the locks gates, all fifteen of them. Even the Captain was impressed and let the lad steer out of the last lock and into the Sound of Jura, having acquired the case of furniture off the dockside at Crinan, bound for delivery to Colonsay.

It was here the weather suddenly changed for the worse.

First the brightness of the day faded in the presence of thick, bruised clouds swept in on a cold wind. Soon rain was splattering and hissing on the funnel and the 'Kelpie' braced herself for rougher waters ahead.

"We will not be going through the gulf of Corryvrechan," shouted the Captain over the growing growl of the sea, "Up and round Scarba will do for us in this weather."

Edward soon gave up on trying to scrub the decks and went to the side to be sick into the angry grey waters beneath the hull.

Mr McGhee stayed fast in the engine room until Edward joined him to add coal to the boiler, and to get a heat.

Mr Hogg, stayed forward on deck, wrapped in a heavy coat and looking out for other shipping.

As the puffer churned past the north of Jura, sure enough, the deep and turbulent roar of the whirlpool could be heard above the howling wind and rain, grinding trapped water and air into mist and rage. It would cost them time to skirt the whirlpool, but the decision had been a sound one.

As the weather deteriorated further bringing more violent waves crashing onto the hull of the boat, it was then decided to anchor in the Shuna Sound by Luing till the storm passed. Captain Nimmo wet a finger in his mouth and placed it above his head for a second, "Aye, it will blow over in a few hours," he declared. "so, we won't be really losing too much time then."

With considerably calmer waters now around the boat, the crew headed off to sleep till the sudden storm from the west had abated.

"What's that giant bird coming over the mountain there?" enquired Edward, as he stood aft on the puffer, looking into the clear, sun-sparkled hills beyond.

"That, son," replied the engineer, "Is a golden eagle, and an omen of good fortune. . . . so," he concluded, "We should all be very glad to have seen it. Now say your wish and ask for blessings quickly before it flies out of view."

Edward did so, quite sincerely, which touched the older man, causing him a wipe away a tear with the rag held in his hand.

The Captain looked long towards the departing eagle, passing out to sea, and felt a pang of transition, the omen to him was not a good one, but not a bad one either, it was an odd feeling of something different.

The sail westwards across to Colonsay was achieved on calmer, steady water, which Mr McGhee claimed was the eagles blessing, and Edward agreed.

As the 'Kelpie' drew into Scalasaig pier, it seemed that the whole Island had turned out to meet them, but despite generous offers of food and beer, which the Captain was very tempted to accept until the First Mate intervened, they quickly readied the vessel again for departure, shifting some of the remaining load in the hold for better keel balance. With several crates now unloaded, and the hold of the puffer rearranged, the pier-master verified the opinion of the First Mate by advising a hasty departure due to the anticipated second wave of incoming Atlantic storm.

Running south east, and with the approaching storm blowing the 'Kelpie' a little faster though her churning wake, the crew buckled down for a rough passage across the Sound Of Islay, and they were well forewarned for the need of a speedy and secure docking at the Distillery.

As the grey walls of Bunnahabhain appeared into view ahead of them, its warehouse walls guarding the shore like a fortress, the chasing storm hit hard, lurching the puffer fore and aft, port and starboard, making her pitch and yaw, challenging the integrity of her hull which held firm against the battering, as it always did.

Docking at the pier was hazardous, but thanks to one of the Distillery workers running down to catch the ropes, and make fast the moorings around the bollards, the puffer was soon secure. The crew disembarked quickly, running up to the distillery for shelter, tea, and some hospitality.

The captain stayed aboard a little longer, and having found where he had left them last, dropped some additional roped tyres over the side of the boat to cushion the hull against hitting the piers stout posts. Happy that the 'Kelpie' would suffer no additional damage from the force of the churning, frothing waves, he pulled his coat collar as high as he could and made his way towards the distillery.

The place was quiet and peaceful, save for the outside blasts of wind and rain on the roof above him, and as he walked slowly towards the growing sound of laughter and the hiss of a boiling kettle, he passed through Bunnahabhains still room where the waft of spirituous malted barley and hot copper warmed him. The burnished brass still safe beckoning him onwards like a found chest of gold. He gazed for a few minutes at the cooled liquor inside the windowed brass box, pouring out the tarnished tap and into a green-stained waiting glass bowl, feeding onwards into the collecting tanks, and for a moment he felt something start to change in his awareness, he felt the presence of the eagle again, flying through clearer skies from out of a troubled storm.

It was sudden, and caught him unaware, causing tears to wet his eyes, he shivered in the heat of the room, brushed his face, and his thoughts turned again to the howl of the storm outside, as if it too had brought him, Norrie Nimmo, Master of the 'Kelpie', a message from the sea.

He shivered again, despite the heat, then braced himself to enter the canteen where the crew were making merry over fresh tea and a packet of biscuits.

"I'm Marky, the warehouse man, here at Bunna," grinned their host.

"Welcome to Islay and welcome ashore. You won't find a better destination on the west coast to hide from a storm," he continued as he poured each of them tin mugs of dark, steaming tea.

"Sugar and milk for anyone then?" he enquired.

Standing six feet tall Marky had milky blue-grey eyes, and a fringe of short mouse-brown hair above a cheerful and unassuming face. His broad shoulders and powerful arms over a stocky frame gave him the appearance of someone bigger, and many years of team rugby as his passion had given him the right build for rolling and stacking casks around warehouses, along with the other jobs he had to do.

As it was late in the evening, and as darkness would be falling soon, Marky offered the crew a berth for the night on the canteen floor as it was the warmest place beside the still room, and had access to a toilet. The crew appreciated his thoughtfulness, and on production of a small bottle of clear spirit from out of a tin bucket he had brought into the room, the crew appreciated him even more.

"Thank you kindly for your valuable help down on the jetty Marky," said the Captain, "And as soon as the storm has passed, which won't be long according to the clouds, we will be loaded and on our way, but, in the meanwhile, we'll be happy to accept your hospitality for the night."

Dinner was baked beans on toast with a couple of poached eggs on top. This was a feast to young Edward, and there was much laughter at his expression of disbelief as he was offered a second helping of beans.

"There you are 'fella," said Marky as what was left in the pan was tipped onto Edward's plate.

"I don't quite place your accent my friend," declared the First Mate, wiping the tea leaves from the rim of his mug, "Liverpool?", he paused, "Lancaster?", "Blackpool?" he added, trying to narrow down the strangers accent.

"Isle of Man," responded Marky, "So I'm Manx and proud of it, and so's you know, a boat brought me here a couple of years ago, and a boat will be taking me away again soon."

Edward tried a taste of the clear liquor, and much to everyones' amusement, spat it out into his plate, and reached quickly for his tea. "Seventy two percent," stated Marky, grinning, and then laughing with the seafarers at the young lads discomfort, after which they promptly toasted the boys loss of innocence, and thereafter, topping up for another dram although Edward's dram was well watered so save further distress.

The following morning delivered a vibrant sun in a clear blue sky, with a gentle, mild wind blowing soft and sweet, charged with a freshness gifted by the departed tempest.

A system was soon organised with Marky rolling out a stream of empty casks from behind the cooperage, passing the barrels one by one to the first mate who rolled them down to the pier, where the engineer took over lashing the casks one by one onto the derrick which the Captain then swung across into the boat with the help of the steam-powered winch.

After being deposited carefully into the ships hold, Edward, with his agility and nimble fingers, would unbind the ropes, shuffling the casks tightly together as best he could, to save on space.

The young man was certainly finding his sea legs now, and the crew noted that he was growing stronger and brighter for it too.

"Being September, it's the dry season and with the river running low. . . so this week is the last stilling for a while and the beginning of maintenance month so they can get all the paint and repair jobs done," stated Marky, grateful that the monotony of their chore was now over after several hours of repetitively hard work. "That's why it's so quiet this morning, oh, and by the way, I'm coming with you to Jura to deliver them if that's ok. . . what? Did nobody tell you?" he grinned.

The warehouseman headed off to close down the stills and collect a large travel bag and a rugby ball before shortly reappearing to join the crew in helping to push off the 'Kelpie' from the Distillery pier and into the swift streaming waters of the Sound of Jura.

Soon they steamed past Caol Ila, belching its tangy peat smoke and full of activity, and continued, due south down, and round Brosdale Island, the 'Kelpie' chuffing contentedly north-east with Craighouse soon homing into view, tucked between Port Na Birlinne and the Small Isles.

Marky was first ashore, drawing admiring glances from the ladies on the quayside as he rolled up his sleeves and organised the crew, including the Captain, into unloading casks onto the pier, where a waiting team of local lads and distillery workers rolled the barrels uphill to the distillery a few yards up the road. With their lorry broken, the puffer delivering straight to their doorstep had been invaluable.

Captain Nimmo was the last to step ashore, looking thoughtful for a while into the boats hold, now hollow and empty.

He finally headed up the few steps towards the distillery door, where laughter and cheery banter floated out with the smell of fine malt whisky, and joined his crew just in time to hear Marky giving his farewell speech to Bunnahabhain.

"I love the people and the Island, but that manager they've got at Bunna is a total bastard, typical ex-military arsehole, and has no reason to be. . . thinks everyone's a conscript on Islay," his face briefly becoming sullen, "Anyways, thanks for the skeet, and all the parties, and for pointing me out that job in Glasgow, I start next week, and it's looking a lot better than where I was."

After a dram or two shared by the crew, Edward, who had volunteered to stay on lemonade for safety, helped the cheery crew along with their guest back down to the dock, then, with the Captain having been reminded three times in as many minutes, as to their final destination, the 'Kelpie' slipped her moorings once more, and puffed back out into the Sound of Jura, heading due south-east towards Loch Stornoway.

The sky was clear, the day was calm, the soft breeze was full of life, and the air it carried was awash with a warming gentleness, the boat easing her way slowly through the sparkling waters beneath the endless sky floating above, and with no hurry to reach a destination, and caught in her brief moment of timelessness.

Marky grinned to the engineer, who chuckled at his plan.

"Oy! Edward, mate . . . will you get a bucket o' steam from the engine room so's I can clean my rugby ball? . . . it's the only thing that shines it up."

Edward duly obliged and reappeared a minute later with a metal bucket covered with an oily old rag.

"Sorry mate, that steams too dry, it's not wet enough for the job!" declared Marky sympathetically, "Could you get me some wetter steam?"

Edward stood frowning, as if in thought, then asked the bigger man a serious question,

"Are you just taking the piss out of me 'cos I'm wee, and you think I'm stupid?"

"Yes!" replied Marky.

The puffer erupted with laughter, except for Edward who, once the laughter has subsided, told Marky that he was just a big shite.

At last, the dazzling white sands of Loch Stornoway Bay loomed like a smear of butter on the horizon.

The Captain paused, assessing the play of the tide ahead, its change from surge to ebb, steering the 'Kelpie' strategically into position whilst still well off-shore, then with the engine murmuring below her decks, the boat skipped easily over the shallow submerged rocks and at last slid with a sigh, and a rush of shifting sand onto the idyllically sparkling, sun-drenched beach.

After careful appraisal, it was agreed that she was indeed, securely beached, and as the tide was on the ebb, would look perfect for the wedding reception guests, expectantly waiting up at the grand house in Carse.

Mr Nicholson's silhouette appeared over the dunes beyond the dusty sand, walking towards the 'Kelpie' with a grin of approval on his face.

"My, but I must say, you've done a fine job of beaching her Captain Nimmo, . . . now will you all come up to the house for sandwiches and some drink," he added, walking round the hull of the vessel, admiring yet again for himself the neat simplicity and function expressed within her form.

The crew dropped the boats ladder over the bows and one by one, descended onto the soft sand below, with only the Captain remaining behind to 'tidy up a bit' before joining the others.

As the excited voices of the crew of the 'Kelpie' began to disappear over the dunes, Captain Norrie Nimmo surveyed his charge, and headed aft to his wheelhouse to roll another cigarette. Looking up into the sky above, he saw an eagle spin and wheel slowly on the coastal breeze, and with it he felt a shiver of pain.

It was over.

It was done.

It was time.

Norrie wandered up towards Carse House, nestled half a mile up the hill, visible between sheltering trees. As he approached the imposing building, hearing the merriment and cheer of the guests and his crew, he stopped, paused, listened again, then finally, and after some consideration, turned away, walking back down to the road, then turning left, wandered along to Ardpatrick where his cousins lived.

They would put him up for a few nights until he had fully considered his future.

It was alright for the Cal Mac officers who had a good pension, but as a puffer commander, his lower commission would leave him fending for himself, but he would manage, he always had.

He stopped for a moment on the silent road and looked again into the sky. He could see the eagle again, high up and wheeling under scattering clouds, circling and banking within the ruby glow of another setting sun, and after pausing to let it all sink in, Norrie finally let some tears arrive to wash away the hurt.

He did not want the change, but fate had decreed, and he understood that it would be foolish to deny, and to try and resist.

The darkness of night was beginning to creep cross the hills ahead of him, but he took the time to roll another cigarette, light it, and enjoy it. His thoughts turned to the little old cottage tucked just down the road from his cousins' house.

It would need a lot of work to make it ready for the winter, but he had bought it the previous year for a modest price. After restorations and repair the cottage would be as warm and cosy as a still room. She would have a sign on the front gate, hand painted by himself, that would welcome visitors to 'Kelpie's Rest'.

Chuckles.

- how a great looking plan can go horribly wrong, and why nothing is learned from experience when your greedy.

Benbow Bunting was a superficially affable fellow, which nature had, purely by default, granted the gift of a disarming cheery grin on his rotund and ruddy face, when he needed it.

His portly physique accentuated the sense of cheerfulness, allowing him to leave a positive impression on most who met him for the first time, a circumstance reinforced by his regular oily-sounding chuckles that littered conversations.

Despite otherwise having a rather bland personality, which many would have regarded as dull and conformist, Benbow, or Benny, as he preferred to be called, was civil company, if somewhat calculating, manipulative, and conceited, once you got to know him better.

His success in life had been steady and modest, having made a career as an insurance company loss adjuster, starting his first office job almost from the moment he left school.

Offices suited him, he could sit in comfort and analyse, scrutinise and adjust by formality and cunning, which, along with his enthusiasm to save his employers money, and to provide claimants with less compensation, made him successful at his job.

A house in Bearsden, a wife, an Italian car, golf club membership, and foreign holidays twice a year, plus frequent weekend meals out in Glasgow, were the trophies for loyalty to his lifestyle.

Life was good despite his nagging health issues of psoriasis, high blood pressure, and acid reflux, for which he took Gaviscon tablets.

The stretch on finances to secure a mortgage for his detached villa in Bearsden had, he considered, been well worth it in the long run as a desirable address was always a house more easy to sell when the time came to do such a thing, but more importantly, the location reflected his ambitions in life.

Money was always a bit tight as it was always spent quickly, and sometimes on a bottle of single malt whisky for special occasions, usually Macallan or Lagavulin.

His best friends birthday was one such occasion, and Barry Bond, chubby, cheery, balding insurance sales executive and competent golfer, was always appreciative of a bottle of Macallan from his good friend.

When fellow golf club members were feeling charitable, the two men were known as the 'chuckle twins', but after downing a few drinks on the nineteenth, the two pals were known as the 'Humpty Dumpties'.

They did look rather similar after all, the names sort of suited them.

The day out to Edinburghs Whisky Fringe Festival changed everything.

The tickets had been a prize in the regular golf club charity raffle, raising money for the charity, Penguins Against Cancer, a noble cause indeed, and the 'right sort' of charity, and as Barry had won the prize of two tickets to the whisky festival, and therefore needed a suitable companion, Benny was the perfect choice.

They boarded the train at Queen Street station early on Saturday morning and within the hour, had arrived at Edinburgh Waverley, having already has a few wee swigs out of the hip flasks concealed within the pockets of their golf slacks.

Topped off with colourful Pringle sweaters and matching golf caps, all that was missing were the putters.

Barry led the way down Broughton Street towards the old church where the event was taking place, and as they approached, they were surprised to find a lengthy and civil queue had already formed, although the festival was not due to commence for another fifteen minutes.

There was a bit of muttering between them about 'standing around for too long', but the crowd were cheery, and a few seemed quietly affluent, which impressed the two pals, who were avid people-watchers.

As soon as they finally got into the ornate hall containing the whisky event, Benny and Barry split up taking one side of the hall each in order to find the table with Macallan, their main focus of malt-enquiry, and plans were already in place to monopolise the stand and get through as many different Macallans as possible without appearing greedy. Other malts were not as important, so any whisky suitable for slipping discreetly into their empty whisky flasks would be coming from the Macallan table. As they re-joined at the end of the hall, faces crest fallen, they had to admit that they could not find the Macallan stand, which was simply ridiculous, with it being the best malt.

Barry looked around, an empty glass still in his hand, spied a rum stand over in the left-hand corner behind the alter.

"How about some rum to start with then Benny, just to wet the whistle?"

"Oh my god," spluttered his friend, "Surely you can't be serious mate, rum? . . . Rum?"

Barry kept silent, absorbing the rebuke, "Listen! . . . we are only going for the best stuff, the old stuff, the expensive stuff, so forget the rum, that's made for mixing with coke anyway, I'm surprised they wasted valuable space on inferior spirits," Benny chuckled, sarcastically.

Barry pointed to the Glenfarclas table, "That stuff looks dark and fruitcake-y, how about there?"

At the table, dressed neatly in a tartan cloth and an array of age-stated bottlings, both the men accepted a sample of the fifteen year old malt, along with an explanation by the presenter, a ruddy-faced, and enthusiastic chap called George, of why the flavour was better due to direct-firing of the copper stills which contained rummagers, and as such, the stills needed replaced every thirty years due to wearing out.

As the men quickly finished off their first drams with comments of 'rich and smooth', Benny sensed that this malt was in fact better than his last Macallan, and as such, he offered his glass for a second pour.

George winked at the two and pulled out a bottle of thirty year old Glenfarclas from under the table cloth, pouring a decent measure and suggesting that a bottle of this stuff would sit well at the nineteenth hole. It was languid, rich, and immensely flavoursome.

"Oh my!" exclaimed Barry, "That's just fabulous, what do you think of it, Benny?"

Benny did not initially reply, transfixed as he was with the age statement and substance of his whisky.

"It's rather good actually, lovely, long-lasting, and smooth!"

In appreciation of the malt, Barry offered one of his limericks to George, for which he felt he had a talent.

"The thoughts of a rabbit on sex," he quipped,

"Are seldom, if ever, complex,

For a rabbit in need,

Is a rabbit indeed,

And does just as a person expects."

"Boom! Boom!" he concluded.

George blushed and laughed, as the two pals chuckled their appreciation for the dram and the limerick, then headed off chuckling, to find another recognisable and smooth-tasting malt.

After sampling a few rounds of whiskies, from various distillers and bottlers, and with time moving on, it was Barry who spotted the Glengoyne table, and ushered his friend towards it for another.

"Oh! Benny, look, that's just up the road from us, we could visit it for the day and maybe buy stuff for later."

An affable, and informed young lady poured two dark-looking drams into their glasses.

"This," she stated, "Is out new teapot dram, available only at the distillery!"

"My, my darlin' but this is lovely stuff, and so charmingly presented by such a lovely young lady," chuckled Benny, dividing his attention equally between the whisky and the host.

"Only available at the distillery too, so we must make a visit soon. I'm from Bearsden, Chesters Road, just by Thorn Park and the Golf Club. . . you might know it, . . . dear?"

"No, never heard of it," replied their host, swiftly turning her attention to another customer.

Later on, and with the final hour now insight, the two chums sped up their table-bagging and having ensured that their flasks were discreetly and fully refilled, pounced on the nearest table as an announcement was made in the hall that final drams were now being poured.

Barry was tossing back the liquor now, not bothering to taste, whilst Benny made sure to appear more controlled, and visibly so, in his relative modesty, attempting some conversation with the attendant now quickly removing bottles from the table.

Benny asked for a now empty bottle and its wooden case, which the attendant was happy to provide.

The following weekend, Benny pulled the dust cover from his red Alpha Romeo Ti Lusso and roared off down Chesters Road to collect Barry at the golf club car park.

As they wound their way up the Stockiemuir Road towards Glengoyne, Benny was keen to discuss the whiskies from the previous week.

"I made a note of what we had," he paused for effect, "Cost a fortune if we had paid for them in bars," he confided. Then chuckled, "Just amazing value, AND, some were collectable grade too," he chuckled again.

"I looked it up, so we need to get four bottles of that Tea Pot dram stuff 'cos prices will go up you know Barry, up, .. up . . . UP!"

Barry responded with interest, listening intently to what Benny might be suggesting.

"If we could find an expert, a club or something, perhaps we could invest properly!" he concluded.

As they approached Glengoyne, the distillery loomed suddenly round the bend in the road, with the warehouses noticeable first, sitting on the left and looking authentic. To the right, a small, dainty whitewashed distillery stood, picture-postcard and quaint, nestled as it was, between steep sloping, tousled, woodland glades. A distinctive, steep hill loomed high above, casting an imposing presence over the buildings below.

"We should climb that one day," stated Barry.

Benny looked up the slope, "I doubt it!" he replied.

In the Distillery, the tour was engaging and thorough, covering the full process and ending in a dram of the ten year old, unpeated malt.

Their guide, an older, grey-haired chap called Duncan, had been roped in to take an additional tour due to a recent coach party of Scandinavian tourists taking longer than anticipated in the blenders suite, and although Duncan knew little about collectable values, he knew plenty about mashing, distillation and cask influence.

Benny thoroughly enjoyed the experience, sensing that something was morphing in his life, something significant, empowering, important.

He asked a lot of questions and showed appreciation for the honest answers he received from Duncan.

Barry, of course, as appreciation for the tour, offered Duncan a limerick for a laugh, which Duncan, with a grin, readily agreed to hear.

"There once was once a plumber called Lee," chortled Barry,

"Who was plumbing a girl by the sea,

She said, "stop your plumbing",

"I think someone's coming,"

Said the plumber, still plumbing, "It's me."

"Boom! Boom!" he concluded.

The three men erupted with laughter, and after a few moments, to allow Duncan to wipe the tears from out of his eyes, they then headed through to the now vacated blenders suite for a final wee dram.

Within the wood-lined walls of the room, bottles glistened under the spotlights above, and glasses stood like soldiers on parade across the polished wooden table.

Duncan poured the two guests a small measure of seventeen year old Glengoyne, and patiently accepted the increasingly probing questions delivered by Benny.

"What's the most expensive bottle ever sold by Glengoyne?"

"What is the mark-up on a cask, and is it worth buying a cask?"

"What's the most 'collectable' bottling in value?"

Duncan patiently addressed all these questions, and more, as best he could, and by the end of the tour, both Benny and Barry had spent almost seven hundred pounds in the shop on what amounted to a full case of bottles.

In the car going back down the road to Bearsden, Benny remained silent most of the way, allowing Barry, who had drunk more, to mumble some whisky trash-talk.

Benny had other thinks on his mind. Duncan had mentioned the 2000AD bottling, packaged in its very own metal spirit safe box, and as it was a good single malt, and as it was increasing rapidly in value as a collector's item, and as it was a fail-proof investment, Benny did the arithmetic in his head, and decided there and then, that he would invest properly in single malt whisky.

Something distracted him from his thoughts, his Alpha Romeo had shuddered slightly and started speeding up, and he immediately recognised the symptom of a recurring problem which had harassed him since buying the car the previous year. The cruise control software was playing up again, he really should get it sorted by the dealership, when he found the time to do so. He reverted to manual override.

Back at the golf club, the two friends, box in hand, entered the bar to allow Barry to show-off their purchases.

Whilst Barry warbled on to the barman about the thrill of the extra samples due to generosity at the distillery, Benny chatted about what he had discovered about whisky-making and the permutations of cask maturation to another couple of the club regulars, who showed both interest and some admiration for Bennys enthusiasm.

It was one of the other, passing regulars, Mrs Niven, slim, well groomed, full of business and often quite officious, who intervened on overhearing the men's conversation.

"I take it you would be interested in joining a whisky club, Mr Bunting? Perhaps Mr Bond would pair with you, and if you like I can make an introduction," she added. "I think you might be accepted after scrutiny, as they are looking for new members…of a certain 'type' of course, so as not to risk the sort of behaviour that members of the public might bring to the clubs reputation."

"They just want to be discreet and exclusive," she added, and Benny liked the sound of what he heard. There were other whisky clubs in Glasgow, but, with better clubs came better drams and better contacts, and that made sense.

It was late when Benny got home, and as he reversed into his driveway, he reminding himself to get the car back to the dealership for warranty repairs as soon as he could, so as to fix the cruise control problem.

Shuffling round to the boot, he removed what was left of the case of Glengoynes and carried the bottles quietly into the garage, making sure they did not clink together and alert his wife to more alcohol entering their home.

In the kitchen, a fresh purple sticky note was attached to the fridge door, held in place by a magnet, gifted by friends travelling in Thailand, a tiny surfboard, and as it caught his attention, he wondered briefly how his friends were doing.

The note read:

OUT TO PILATES TONIGHT,

BACK LATE, DON'T WAIT UP/LOVE YOU.

He chuckled to himself, wait up? He shook his head, he never waited up for her these days, that was history now, and he knew she would not be leaving anytime soon, as the quality of life was too good to let go. He knew it, and she knew it too!

He retired to his studio at the back of the house and settled down with a tumbler and the now opened bottle of teapot dram, and poured a large splash, chuckling to himself at the enjoyment of his successful visit to Glengoyne, and after a few hours of listening to Dizzy Gillespie, then Miles Davis through his Bang And Olufsen headphones, he headed off to bed, with half the bottle of single malt now resting within his tummy.

The wife was not home yet, but no matter.

The following week, Benny picked up a sealed magnolia coloured envelope from reception at the golf club.

He was already feeling pleased with himself having driven to Oddbins and other better quality retailers over the last few days to purchase over twenty bottles of Macallan and Lagavulin, as these were clearly the foundations of any reputable, and profitable whisky collection.

The message was nicely handwritten, with an embossed letterhead stating:

'West End Malt Circle'

'Devonshire Gardens'

and it concluded beneath the small and tasteful watercolour image of a stags head,

'Exclusively inclusive'.

It read,

'Dear Benbow,

Following a satisfactory introduction from our friends at Bearsden Golf Club, and on behalf of our Malt Circle, I am directed by committee to extend an invitation to both yourself and to Mister Bernard Bond, to join us for better acquaintance on Friday 13th October at the address above, commencing eight p.m.

I'm sure you will find us agreeable company.

Yours faithfully

Major Findlay M. MacIntosh Esq: DSO

Please note, formal dress.

R.S.V.P.

Benny shivered in excitement, and rushed to reception for pen and paper, ensuring that the paper he received was the headed version, thicker weight, and with a firmer envelope.

He delivered the sealed message by hand to the Malt Circle venue, a discreet location at the beginning of Devonshire Gardens, Hyndland, near the crossroads, and very appropriate.

Benny felt at home there, it was classy.

When Friday the 13th arrived, the two men made sure that it was a traditional black hackney cab taxi which dropped them off at the stone arched porch of the Malt Circle venue, and a brisk and sprightly balding man with a clipped black moustache opened the door to allow entry for the immaculate black-tied chums.

"I say, lovely to meet you, do come on in chaps," cooed their host, Major MacIntosh.

The major offered his right hand in welcome, and Benny felt that the firmness and press of the Majors thumb into his knuckles, as they shook hands, may have had some significance, but he was not sure.

Leading the way up a short flight of broad, carpeted stairs, the three entered a large reception room.

"So, are you affiliated to a lodge at all," quipped the Major breezily turning round to address Benny, "Oh, no, I think the Lodges are too aggressive, what with all the flute bands blocking the streets every year in marching season." he responded, hoping it was an appropriate reply.

The Major just grinned and gestured towards a rather large dark polished oak table at the centre of the room surrounded by about twenty practical, but heavy looking seats.

"Honourable members," he declared, "please make welcome our distinguished guests."

There was a generous round of clapping in the room from all those assembled, after which champagne was offered to the two men, which they accepted with due grace and murmurs of thank you.

Benny and Barry both felt the thrill of opportunity.

The following day at the golf club, Barry and Benny sat chatting with Mrs Niven in a more discreet corner of the bar. "So! . . . tell me all about it then," she demanded.

"You probably noticed that there are no women present at the circle!" she continued, without waiting for their reply, "But, there you go, boys and their toys!" she sighed, turning her attention back to the two men at across the table.

"The Major was very civil and pleasant to be honest," stated Barry, looking nervously towards his friend, "And Sir Myles was cheery the whole night, along with his pals Dudley and that civil servant fellow, who . . . well . . . I forget his name now."

Benny picked up on the thread, "The labour M.P. was a bit formal and you can see he does not really like the Major, and the two members of the 49 Wine and Spirits Club were rather aloof, sticking to themselves, and talking business." he concluded, "But I never really noticed anything stand-out about the rest, perhaps it was because we were all dressed similarly."

Mrs Niven brushed her plum coloured golfing slacks with her hand, lightly dusted her loose fitting Lacoste shirt, narrowed her eyes as if deep in thought for a few seconds, before responding, "They seemed to like you both. Especially you Benny, with your whisky knowledge. Have you been swotting up young man?" she asked.

He confirmed that he had. In fact, over the last month, Benny had bought no less than seven whisky books to absorb as much relevant information as he could, as quickly as possible. After all, if you were 'in it to win it' knowledge was power, and power was profit, although most of the books repeated the same information, focussing on individual distillery technicalities.

Benny found himself memorising the singular identifying characteristics of smell and taste as this seemed good to disclose in conversation. It made one look informed.

"Well then," declared Mrs Niven, "Good luck to you both, and remember, you are ambassadors of my clubs reputation, so don't get drunk or do anything silly out there, . . . or else! I know what happens round here boys, so keep the end up, won't you!"

The two boys agreed, and Mrs Niven then got up to retire back to the office for another squint at the security cameras. She hated when kids ran across the green, stealing golf balls and such, they were almost as bad as the rabbits.

Before the next meeting of the Malt Circle, Benny bought a lot more whisky, and acquired a lot more information. Online research was useful for this, and he quite liked Whiskyfun, as the notes were comprehensive, and the range of bottlings reviewed, unsurpassed.

It was the right *sort* of website.

Whiskybase was useful too, to cross check that smell and flavour references were similar, so as he did not describe anything out of character when discussing a malt, and so that his descriptors conformed to the norm, the agreed patterns.

YouTube videos were useful too, although many reviewers were not to his liking, especially one called 'ralfy' who he found to be a long-winded arsehole. In fact, 'ralfy' irritated him a lot, as this reviewer was clearly not the 'right sort' and he had non-conformist opinions. However, as ralfys higher-marked reviews clearly influenced a lot of whisky purchases, especially when the mark given was over ninety out of a hundred, then there was a chance that the whisky reviewed would be worth investing in as a reliable financial asset.

He kept smell and taste references short, with 'breakfast tea', 'fruity', 'vanilla', 'dark chocolate', and 'deep rasin-y' as favourite references. Adjectives were useful, with 'impressive', 'characterful', 'energetic', 'smooth', unique, and of course, 'amazing'.

'sherry', and 'bourbon-y' were always useful as he would try to check on the cask first anyway so as not to get it wrong. It did not take him long to get the knack of conventional whisky-talk.

Over the next few months, Benny's reputation steadily grew within the realm of the Malt Circle.

Even the two from the 49 Club started chatting to him, and he was cordially invited to passenger a car in the HeroEvents Rally, after all, he had an Alpha Romeo, which was sort of appropriate.

He accepted of course, on condition it was the Scottish highland section, through distillery country.

Despite anticipation, he did not enjoy the experience as the driver of the E-type Jag in which he was a passenger was an idiot from the moment they left the start-line, and when the car broke down going over some loose turf at the side of the road, he had been expected to get out and push.

Major Findlay found the situation very amusing, and started to warm a little towards the new club member who was displaying more enthusiasm than his other portly pal, Barry, who had now buddied up at meetings with Sir Myles to get mutually and ambiently drunk at the end of the table.

Benny contributed more, and his knowledge was a useful asset to the Club.

It was Benny who approached Gordon And MacPhail, the largest independent bottlers of scotch whisky and persuaded them to provide the next Club charity tasting, in aid of Help For Heroes.

Usually, with the Clubs status, distillers would willingly provide free bottles and other merchandise, as it was, after all, for good causes, and recipient charities were always happy to connect with Major Findlays largesse. He was good at that sort of thing.

Benny phoned the bottlers the week before the tasting to ensure they were providing appropriate bottlings, and was much relieved to know that they were, as it was something they did frequently for their more 'valued' connects, so they were at ease with the protocols.

It was a few days later, and with the next Malt Circle event only one week away, that Benny arrived home after another lack-lustre day in the office to find a fresh purple sticky note on the fridge door.

'PHONE MR HARRIS, DOWN THE ROAD AT NUMBER 14' it read, with a phone number underlined at the foot of the note.

He poured a tumbler of Talisker 18 first and sipped it a few times, then phoned the number, to be met with a fragile and slightly croaky voice at the other end of the line.

Ahhh!" exclaimed Mister Harris, "Thank you so much Mister Benbow for getting back to me so soon."

"I have heard from friends who play golf locally that you are a whisky expert!" he said, pausing to allow Benny to confirm his status.

"Well, Mister Harris, I would hardly say I'm in Charlie MacLeans league, however, I do have some experience and many good contacts across the Industry, and I am a member of the Malt Circle, . . . you may have heard of it." he chuckled.

Mister Harris had never heard of the Malt Circle, so Benny continued, taking another gulp from his tumbler. "And how may I be of service Mister Harris?"

"I am a retired journalist, and I live just down the road, and I have a few bottles of whisky, sealed of course, which I am looking to sell."

Benny's eyes narrowed and the tumbler was quickly placed down on the table.

The door of Number 14 Chesters Road opened to reveal an emaciated old man, rough shaven, clearly not in the best of health and in his hand, a long cigar, which he seems content to inhale like a cigarette.

He ushered his rotund guest in through the door, glancing out for possible passers-by who may have noticed, but there were none to be seen.

They went through to a smoke filled back room of the large, but plainly adorned house, where a studio office was situated, containing, on a couple of shelves, an eclectic array of bottles of scotch whisky.

Benny swiftly counted them, there must have been about thirty bottles, and all of them single malt.

"I want to sell them, but I know nothing about whisky", whined the old man.

"Are you, well, you know, interested in any of them?"

Benny perused the array, a Sherriffs 7yo Bowmore, Cadenheads 1975 Ardbeg, Macallan 25yo, a St Magnus Label Highland Park pure malt, Laphroaig 12yo prime malt, and many other, mainly Islay whiskies from the nineteen fifties through to the nineteen eighties.

All were in mint condition.

"Er, Huh, Ah," chuckled Benny to cover his shock,

"Why are you selling them?" he asked.

The old man just sighed, "I was a journalist, food, drink, agriculture, at the Glasgow Evening Post for most of the time, then did freelance for the Scottish Field and English magazines who wanted Scottish content, so, obviously, the distilleries gave me gifts, with me being the press, it was the perks of the job, everybody did it, and still do it now, but," he continued, "I hate whisky, gins my thing, gin and cigars," he laughed briefly and weakly, before a nasty hacking cough took over, convulsing him for a few moments.

Benny waited patiently.

"I just want rid of them now!" the old man concluded, sighing.

"So, how much are you looking for?" chuckled Benny, the warmth making him start to blush.

"Oh, I dunno… maybe…well. . . What do you think they are worth? You are the expert. I can't be bothered with all the hassle at auction houses."

"Well," countered Benny, "considering the condition and wear and tear, and fading on the labels,", he paused, gauging the old man's expression, which did not change.

"Hows about five hundred pounds."

he old man brightened up, "Fantastic, I can get a few more bottles of gin at the supermarket now."

Benny only shared part of the purchase details with the Major at the next Malt Circle, and on hearing that it was in fact a journalist who sold the bottles, the Major seemed pleased with Bennys windfall.

The HelpForHeroes Tasting was a huge success, with splendid malts and good commentary from the presenter, an experienced and knowledgeable guide, who fitted in well despite his background.

Over five hundred pounds was collected afterwards and presented to the Major to pass on to the M.O.D.

Sir Myles was overtly drunk, and clearly enjoying the limericks that Barry was happy to share, "Boom! Boom!" could be heard occasionally across the room, quickly followed by another cascade of laughter. It was a good night.

Bennys next move was to suggest that perhaps if the Robertson Trust were to be beneficiaries of the next Malt Circle meet, then Macallan might put up the malts, and even one of their blenders might present the whiskies.

The Major thought this a splendid idea, as he knew managers at the Edrington Offices, and as they would be meeting at Blair Castle that weekend for a Quaich Event, he would chat them round to it.

Benny sat shivering in excitement in his kitchen, then poured another GlenDronach 15yo, which, as it was all the rage at the moment, he had cash-handed a local retailer to sell him four sealed cases, which were now in his garage along with all the other assorted cases of scotch. The car had to stay outside on the drive these days. Benny liked to sit in a deckchair in his garage and guess how much his collection would be worth in a few years. It made him happy, especially when he was drinking on his own.

Mz Carberry-Jung had just phoned, a master blender from Edrington, in charge of the malts portfolio, and clearly, obviously, a significant person. She had just phoned *him*, Benny Bunting, whisky expert and collector, and he chuckled at the memory of what she had just said, that she had heard of him as a prominent ambassador for scotch whisky and obviously, off the record of course, nomination as a 'Keeper of the Quaich' was entirely reasonable. The Major thought it a good idea too.

Blair Castle was such a good location. Just perfect, very select.

Benny was ecstatic and chuckled along to another fill-up of GlenDronach, adding plenty of ice to drink it more easily.

The day could not arrive soon enough.

Miss Carberry-Jung was an attractive, classy lady. She presented the 12yo, 18yo, 25yo and 30yo Macallans expertly, then the 'Rare Cask' then the 'Reflexion' expression to round off the evening.

The Malt Circle were enthralled. Benny glanced at the Major, who in turn nodded his approval.

Miss Carberry-Jung asked if there were any questions.

Barry was poked by Sir Myles, and then poked again, until he slurred out a question for the host.

"Tell me, Mz C-J, would you like to hear a limerick?"

Unfazed, Miss Carberry-Jung offered her consent.

Sir Myles was already in fits of mirth, even as Barry delivered his poem.

"There once was a lady named Jill,

Who played with grenades for a thrill,

They found her Vagina,

in North Carolina,

And bits of her tits

in Brazil."

"Boom! Boom!"

Sir Myles erupted in laughter.

At the Malt Circle Committee Enquiry two days later, it was agreed to suspend Barry from the Group, offer a written apology to Eddington, another written apology to Miss Carberry-Jung, and that a charity donation of five hundred pounds from Benny, for the Robertson Trust, be offered in good faith.

Benny could not contain his anger down the phone.

"You absolute, total blithering idiot Barry, I just can't believe what you did, just can't,

can't,

. . can't"

Barry whimpered back down the phone, "It wasn't me Benny, mate, it was the drink!" he explained, then added "Sir Myles put me up to it, dared me I wouldn't do it."

"Never mind Sir Myles, what about my standing in the community, my. . . reputation, you fool, my nomination as a Keeper of the Quaich may be in jeopardy as a result of your stupid, absurd. . . crazy, silliness. Now listen here Barry!" Benny continued , oblivious to his friend now sobbing down the phone, "If you want another Club, try Glasgows Whisky Club in town, where your humour will be better appreciated by the blue-collar brigade", he paused, slowing his delivery, "We don't play golf together for a while now, I will let Mrs Niven know the situation, you can go to the golf club in the morning if they allow you, and I will go in the evening, we don't meet, we don't talk , we don't communicate, not for a while, . . . goodbye!"

Benny sat within the silence of his kitchen, then, after a pause, glanced up to towards the fridge door where a purple sticky note stated in capital letters, WE ARE DIVORCING AND LAWYER WILL CONTACT SOON. LOVE YOU. P.S. CAR NOT WORKING. GET IT FIXED.

He stood up, sighed, and went to the window, looking out onto the wreckage of his Alpha Romeo which was now embedded through the door of the garage, shattering many of the bottles stacked within, creating an ambient but intense odour of paint, petrol, engine oil, and

GlenDronach 15yo, all intermingled with vintage Islay 'peatiness' and some sherried smoke.

He sighed again, and returned to his tumbler, where the recently opened bottle of Macallan would have to be emptied before he retired to bed.

Right enough, he thought, things happen in threes. He chuckled, then filled his glass, adding ice and shaking the glass to help it become a little smoother. It was a lovely colour, fruity and, yes, definitely, . . . smooth.

The Year is 1824

- how we need to know history to understand history and to learn from history.

The pain in his leg was getting worse. A lot worse. Donald had to lean harder on the stout reins of his old pony Fuchrean, who patiently plodded onwards and upwards along the overgrown track, towards the bend in the Corriearklet burn, nestled discreetly below the rolling crags of the mountain called Maol Mor.

The wetter weather and the chill of the oncoming winter brought with it an intense ache from the old wound received at Waterloo that worsened with every passing year.

He had walked with a limp for the best part of a decade now. Greying rapidly, emaciated, wrinkled, and slightly stooping, despite being still in his early fifties, the weight of a hard and troublesome life made him look older than his years.

Donald had accepted the shilling of King George after the recruiting sergeant had bought him ale in a bar in Stirling, and then another sergeant demanded the shilling back later, as payment for his uniform. He was in Belgium by then, with no way home, and the threat of beatings if he did not comply.

Like so many of the men around him, Donald could not have imagined the maelstrom of what became known as the Battle of Waterloo. He fought, was wounded, and survived as a damaged man.

On his return to Scotland he found employment as a drover on the West Highland Way, driving the cattle from Oban to Glasgow for the Duke of Montrose.

He liked the job. The pay was poor but sufficient for his needs. He was left alone with none but cattle for company, and the clear, clean winds of the rugged landscape he walked within, to blow away some of the hurt of his past life. But, while much of the distress of the war decreased over time, the physical distress from the bullet that was still lodged above his knee, increased. Donald had been lucky perhaps, that the field surgeon had been too busy to tend to him properly since it was so much quicker and easier to amputate the leg than it was to remove a musket ball.

However, Donald did not feel lucky now, and as the leg got worse his droving days were numbered. It was finally agreed that he should tenant a small croft by Loch Arklet and make aqua vitae for the Duchess who frequented the lodge at Inversnaid during the short, summer months.

The duchess was by now well tired of London and the routine of court and preferred to make increasingly more time for the freshness and simplicity of highland life.

The situation suited Donald well, he was left alone, and proved to be a very capable distiller, providing a consistent, reliable, and sweet liquor for the lodge kitchen. In fact, so highly was Donalds skill on the pot regarded, that he also sold small casks to The Inn at Inverarnan, and to the warden at the Ardlui Estate. His main outlet however was the farmer at Balmaha, at the foot of Loch Lomond. Here he swapped the liquor for cash and pot-ready grain. The shrewd farmer saw that the highland 'uisce-beatha' fetched a good coin from Glasgow, where demand was strongest, and so prices were good.

Donald could always pay his rent on time and due to his skills and general usefulness he was a welcome addition to the community.

The only discord to this agreeable situation came when his younger cousins were suddenly evicted by the local laird from their small hut up on Rannoch Moor, to make room for grazing sheep and deer. As they headed south to Glasgow to find work, they stayed the night with Donald and it was agreed that the two boys, James, who was eleven, and Malcolm, who was seven, should stay with their uncle Donny as they would have shelter and food, things that could not be guaranteed in Glasgow.

The two lads were happy with the situation although, at first, Malcolm cried bitterly when he realised that mother and father had gone without him. Donald had to settle him and his older brother down for the night with warm-watered sweetened liquor, infused with soothing herbs.

The two lads made themselves useful, tending the garden crops, fetching and carrying, and feeding and grooming Fuchrean, who rather enjoyed being fussed over, and grew to like the boys a lot.

They were both small, swift, alert, and smart. They quickly learned the pot skills and developed a knowledge of the plants, trees, and landscape around them under Donalds instruction. The older, fair-haired, athletic James, took to distilling readily, never drinking a drop whilst he tended the pot, which was good.

Malcolm, darker haired, delicate, and moody, missed his parents but kept brave, trusting in the comfort of his older brothers more positive outlook.

James was cheekier, and funnier, Malcolm was the quiet, thoughtful one, and the one who needed a more specific purpose in life.

The boys soon settled down and got on with the business of living.

By the time Donald and Fuchrean reached the bend in the Corriearklet, the sound of brisk running water and some shelter from the wind allowed the pony to soften its pace and respond to the hugs and fuss from the two lads who had already seasoned the still and readied a good fifty gallons of fresh boiled, and now cooling wort ready to take the yeast still wrapped in a cool damp cloth.

"Mind and keep a soft and steady heat there James ma' lad," insisted Donald, winking at Malcolm, who was stacking more timber by the side of the dry-stone shed they used as their shelter.

Impregnated with moss and ferns and with a heather-thatched roof, it was big enough for the purpose, and small enough for discretion.

They were rarely troubled by visitors.

It was too remote.

Tea was brewed, shared, and drank, and James then demanded to know another story about Waterloo. Donald was not in the mood with the ache gnawing in his leg, so he swiftly changed the subject to the Lady Caroline, Duchess of Montrose, who, it was claimed had spent five hundred pounds on a dinner set of fine Chinese porcelain which now sat at Inversnaid lodge being polished daily by the maids. The lads gasped at the price, trying to imagine that much wealth and what they would spend it on if they had it …certainly not plates!

Malcolm was further interested, piping up "And does her Ladyship have books too, about stuff and everything?" he asked.

"Aye lad, lots of books bound in softest leather and gold," replied his uncle, reaching to the kettle for a re-fill of warming tea.

The rushing wind rose outside, becoming stronger, and Donald felt that he heard a distant voice carried on the air. James galloped off to check, and after a few minutes returned to confirm that it was just the spirits, the ghosts of the glen. No other human was out there, and all was well.

A storm was surely brewing over the mountains, but Donald was not concerned, it would suit their venture very well to have inclement weather, dark clouds, and a stiff wind too, for the sail down Loch Lomond after the casks had been loaded for transportation.

James volunteered to remain behind to mind the fermenting liquor over its first few hours, allowing his uncle and brother to descend the track, back to their home. Evening was coming in fast, and bringing an early night, and the gloaming at the end of the day was a better time to be moving.

As Donald and Malcolm finished their stew by the fireside, settling for the evening, and conscious of the growing roar of wind bringing the storm behind it, Donald glanced up at the small window facing onto the Loch and was shocked to see the murky shadow of a human face peering in at them.

Shouting to Malcolm to hide fast, he instinctively rushed for his stick and a knife from above the fireplace, and Malcolm screamed in alarm as his uncle threw open the door to confront the intruder.

It was James. A cold, wet, confused and slightly nervous James.

Once they had calmed down, James tearfully apologised for causing the alarm, but was reassured that it was nought but a misunderstanding, and that he should not blame himself.

Donald took out the honey pot and spooned the wild sweetness onto some fresh bannocks to steady the boys and let them know they were safe.

James made it clear that he had dampened the fire, turfing the smouldering logs and then wrapped the pot in a damp blanket to stabilise the fermenting environment as carefully as possible.

Donald was reassured after his check that James has been thorough.

Two days later, when they made their way back up the glen without the pony to find that the pot had fermented out, with the resultant wash, dry, sour, and herbaceous. Donald deemed the results to be perfect, and then he checked other, smaller vessels to see how they had fermented too. The results were not as distinctive but deemed good enough for inclusion in the first pass of the still.

After a few hours and much cheek from the boys, Donald reset the flame and decided that as James has tended the ferment, Malcolm should tend the first stilling.

He agreed reluctantly, but James sat down beside him to advise and encourage his younger brother, as Donald made out and over to the gushing stream to stretch his legs a little.

Malcolms firewood was placed under the battered, bruised copper still and a light smoke quickly filled the stone room, slowly finding its own way up and through the thatch above, where the wind swiftly scattered the remaining threading wisps into the elements and air beyond.

Malcolm controlled the smoke as best he could. Once his brother and uncle had left and made their way back down the track, he settled deep within the small sheltered space to feel the heat from the fire and to tend the first-pass of the still, although he was never at ease with it.

A day later, the three kinsmen examined the casks arrayed outside the still house. Pulling back the turf that covered each of the seven casks to check and sample the soft liquor, stronger than beer but weaker than brandy. It was James turn now to tend the still after it had been filled with the half-liquor. The second run was more dangerous than the first, due to the flammability of the spirit now coming through the condensing worm pipe, and Donald insisted that as James was older, faster, and more trusted not to have an accident, he should mind the run.

James was a natural, and Donald was surprised at the quality that the young lad coaxed from the pot and into the waiting casks. He attributed this to James running a slow fire, then growing it hotter as the feints began pushing over the copper neck and down into the worm coils immersed deep within a moss strewn barrel of cold running stream water, constantly fed, and freshened with more cold water from higher up the stream by a long iron pipe running in though the side wall of the hut.

Within four days, the three liquor-makers had four full, five-gallon casks of market ready spirit - soft, clear and fine of flavour. Fuchrean took the weight of the casks comfortably on his back thanks to a thick blanket under the saddle to spread the load more comfortably.

Donald and the lads went westwards along Loch Arklet and descended steeply, far on the south side of the river Arklet, towards

Loch Lomond. They made their way down through the woods of Inversnaid, keeping clear of the Duchess's Lodge, for fear of alerting residents and staff.

By the Loch, under cover of rocks, was hidden a small single mast rowing clinker with a folded patched red sail and flaking grey paint along her bows. As Donald undid the casks from the pony, the two boys ran into a gorse thicket and then pulled hard on a short rope to manage the boat out of its hiding place and down to the waters edge. Here Donald loaded the casks evenly, then wrapped the rowlocks tightly with hessian cloth to muffle his oars and so to make for stealthier progress down the Loch.

Waving goodbye to James and Malcolm, Donald watched a while as the two lads nimbly returned up the woodland along with Fuchrean and out of his sight. He paused to catch the direction of the wind, then after pulling hard on the oars to get away from land, he then paused to hoist the sail as soon as he was able to do so safely.

It was getting dark now, and with the use of moonlight, he navigated the Loch southwards using the dark silhouette of surrounding hills and mountains, which were more dependable than missing starlight.

It was a long haul, heading southwards down Loch Lomond, and he made sure to keep to the land on his left where there were far fewer watching eyes.

Donald enjoyed these moments on the water, letting his aching leg rest when under sail, or rowing rhythmically on the oars, alone, undisturbed and with a feeling of raw freedom which was very precious to him and which he treasured deeply.

As he passed by the shadow of Ben Lomonds rolling, lofty summit, Donald was suddenly aware of soft un-earthly voices, remote sighs and whispers, floating towards him on the air, and they followed him onwards as far as the Rowardennan Lodge before being blown away on a sudden, colder wind passing briskly down the water. He was both puzzled and slightly alarmed at the event, which he had experienced on previous voyages, but not with the intensity he had had on this night.

Something was different.

As the journey was around fifteen nautical miles, he was grateful for the sail, which, with a north-westerly wind blowing gently behind it, carried him easily and silently through the night.

Softly tacking onwards, he reached the tall reed covered entrance of the Endrick water, where, within the cover of the rivers banks, he at last moored, just as dawn was breaking over the fields of Gartfairn Farm, the farm being home to Mr and Mrs Smith, well known and notorious traders of highland aqua vitae to quality ale houses in Glasgow . . . amongst other business interests.

He waited silently, but after an hour, when the parties he expected failed to appear, he left the boat, its cargo now hidden by grass and reeds, and made his way along a small sandy path towards the farm. It seemed different as he approached the farmhouse, and despite the noise of assorted farm animals, it was too quiet of human activity.

Instinctively, he stayed close to the hedges and off the tracks leading to the house, where, as he arrived, saw three well-groomed horses, saddled and tethered at the front gate post.

Beside them stood two red-coated soldiers armed with rifles.

He could smell the danger as he avoided their line of sight and crept closer towards the farmhouse.

Through the open kitchen window, Donald could hear raised voices. One of them he recognised as belonging to Sarah Smith, wife of the farmer, and a stocky, determined woman, who did not suffer fools. The other voice was that of a well-spoken, authoritative man who had the sound of an officer about him. The second voice pricked at his memory and Donald found himself drawn closer to the window.

Suddenly he saw to his horror the face of the man standing by the fireside. Captain Nathanial Gillespie, the villain who merrily shot his own troops on the battlefield of Waterloo to impress the generals with his discipline and leadership. The same officer who sold letters of betrayal to Napoleon. Letters of deceit and of treachery against his own Country and was well rewarded for them with money and favour by the enemy, and by some of his own countrymen too.

A short, obese and chinless, pig-faced man, Captain Gillespie had joined his brother as a tax enforcement officer, a position which gave licence for his instinctive cruelty and the opportunity to abuse the weaker population, and to make money whilst he was at it.

Nathanial along with his brother, Malcolm Gillespie, were known as the most notorious government gaugers in Scotland.

As the tension of the situation within the kitchen rose, a large hound pulled at the heavy chain lead held by Captain Gillespie, growling, snarling and baring its teeth.

As the man grinned and made ready to loose the beast at the farmer's wife standing defensively behind her kitchen table, the woman demanded, again, to know his business.

"Listen woman!" he spat, "Give me money and a barrel and I will be gone for a while, otherwise, my dog will feed on your hands."

"Indeed sir, . . . will he then?" questioned Sarah, swiftly pulling out a pistol from a towel within her flour bin.

With a sudden explosion of gunpowder and sulphurous smoke, the beast lay quivering and dying at the feet of his master, blood seeping softly from a neat round hole between his flickering canine eyes.

"Let loose your hound now . . . Captain Gillespie," added Sarah grimly, laying down the smoking pistol and drawing a second, fresh firearm from the cutlery drawer in front of her.

"It's not the farmer round here you need to fear sir," she roared, "It's the farmer's wife!"

The noise of the gunfire had brought the two soldiers crashing into the room, but Gillespie quickly ordered them to stand down.

There was a moments silence as the Captain stooped to lift his dog from out of the blood in which it now lay, still and dead.

Raising his head, he spat across the table at Sarah, who remained unmoved with her pistol at the ready. His face contorted with fury Gillespie slowly backed himself towards the door hissing to his troops as he did so to get to their horses, sure in the knowledge that Sarah's next bullet would be for him.

As he turned away spitting curses at the women, Captain Gillespie caught sight instead of Donald staring in through kitchen window rigid with shock at what he had seen.

Recognition and hatred burned in the Captain's eyes "Damn you to hell vermin," he roared, "I remember you well from Belgium, you peasant" he exclaimed, "You're the runner who took the evidence of my undoing to General Wellington, and would not take the money offered from Colonel Chumleys' man to hand across the letters against me."

The Captains face was a mask of rage, Sarah and her pistol were forgotten for the moment.

"You were the messenger that destroyed my advancement, and I tell you man!" he paused, his countenance made pale with fury, "there will be a reckoning".

"GET OUT!" roared Sarah, and with one last backward glance, Captain Gillespie, still clutching the dead hound, mounted his horse, and flanked by his men, galloped off towards the Dryman road.

Donald made swiftly into the kitchen to support Sarah, who was now trembling violently, not with nerves, but with rage.

"We are being betrayed again Donald ma' lad," she declared, fussing to boil the kettle over the fire, and to make ready tea and cakes for the two of them. "The gentry get jealous of those below them making a success of themselves, and despite the cut they take, and the money they make, they get greedy, then angry, then spiteful, just to make sure we know our place."

As the tea brewed in the pot, Sarah re-loaded her discharged pistol and placed it back into the flour bin within a fresh towel, to keep it clean.

Smiling briefly, she looked across towards Donald, "I fear that you are now in danger, as although the blaggard will not re-visit soon, he will not be far away, and looking to rob you and even kill you as revenge."

160

She paused, thinking, "Best that you sail north up the middle of the Loch tonight, and avoid all prying eyes, for that devious man will surely be able to buy the gossip and hearsay of locals, as these are hard times."

Donald agreed, and they both sat in silence sipping tea and munching on the fresh baked scones from the oven, until, at last, farmer Smith and his dozen men came clattering in their carts and on their horses, back home down the farm road, fresh from delivery to Glasgow, and holding safe the cash and kind they had received.

Farmer Smith readied the new sacks of malted, kilned, and ferment-ready grain, all harvested from his own fields, and with two of his men, helped Donald load the boat and make ready to set sail as soon as the day was ending, allowing for cover of night. Back in the kitchen, Sarah cooked Donald a fine dinner to stay his hunger and give him strength.

Whilst he ate at the table, she sat and chatted over her beer of her concerns that her husband's cousin George, also a farmer, from the Drummin farm, north of Aberdeen had just taken a licence from the Duke of Gordon to make spirit, legally, under government licence, and free of taxes too. She seemed worried at this development, but unsure of its consequences for them. In truth, in fact, she wished her cousin well, but feared for his safety and that of his family.

That evening, just before the boat was pushed off from the bank of the Endrick water, Donald was handed a loaded pistol, along with eleven more rounds of powder and shot. He knew how to use the weapon, after all, he had been well trained, but even as he set the sail out into the Loch, Donald felt that the gun would not do him any good, in fact, he really preferred to be unarmed, but could not refuse this gift from his benefactor.

Donald rowed quietly, and slowly out from the mouth of the Endrick water, heading north west towards the pass of Balmaha, a route that Sarah had advised him against, but heading out and west round the Isles of Inchcailloch and Inchfad would cost him time and energy, so he kept his original route.

An passing easterly gust caught his attention and gave the opportunity to hoist the sail again and speed progress northwards.

It was still twilight as the vessel slid silently through the pass of Balmaha, a narrow stretch of water between an island and Balmaha village, and Donald relaxed a little as the journey continued uneventful and peaceful.

As he neared the Isle of Inchlonaig, looming dark and low on his port side, he became aware of muffled sound to his right coming from the old earthwork at Strathcashel Point. He suddenly noticed a distant snorting of a horse, which alerted him to the brief small flash of red light coming from the ruins, and immediately, there was a whine of hot lead above him and a neat, scorched hole within the taut sail just above his head.

There was another flash of red, and a splinter of wood cracked up from the gunwale just in front of his seat. The assailants were good shots, too good. He could sense their military discipline.

Swiftly, he pulled the tiller to the right, veering his small boat out and into the Loch, placing the bags of grain behind him as cover and it was not a moment too soon as another ball of whizzing lead blasted into the sacks behind him, scattering some scorched barley grist onto the deck.

With the wind in his favour he set course by the Creagan rock, northwards up the west bank of Loch Lomond, well clear of any further attempts by Gillespie and his men to kill him.

Many hours later, his boat slid silently into its mooring below Inversnaid and Donald quickly dragged to vessel under cover of the rocks and gorse where it would be safe from discovery. He swiftly moved upwards, and into the woods where he lay low until he heard the soft whistle from Malcolm that the boys had arrived with Fuchrean to carry the grain to safety.

The two lads immediately sensed something was wrong and that there was a reason for their uncles late return, but they said nothing until they were back in sight of Loch Arklet and feeling safer.

"What happened uncle?" demanded Malcolm.

"Nothing lad, nothing much, but we need to take cover now, and hide the stills, for there is trouble coming behind us that you don't need to know about for now." he replied calmly.

The two lads asked no more questions till they were back in the bothy and the kettle was hissing steadily on the stove.

Donald thought for a minute as he gazed into the flames of the fireplace, then confided to the boys the happenings at Gartfairn farm, and who Gillespie was, and the history that lay between him and the perverted man on the battlefields of Belgium.

The boys listened silently and attentively without interruption.

"So, you see lads, we now need to lay low, 'till Gillespie loses interest, and moves on to other matters". He spoke confidently but, in his heart, he knew that Gillespie would find a way to seek him out. He was saddened at the thought that the boys had been dragged into something that was none of their concern.

Donald explained what Gillespie had done, in detail, and the two boys were mesmerised at such foul behaviour and contempt for humanity.

"He's a cursed, wretch lads," stated Donald, "And we need to keep out of his way as . . . I know too much."

At first light, Donald surveyed the sky for a weather forecast, and seeing the cloud and mist low over the hills, was reassured that Gillespie and his men would be struggling to get past Rowardennan, as the land was too difficult for horses, too slow for walking, and just too wet for progress.

He knew he had time but not as much as he hoped for.

The three of them along with the pony, made brisk pace uphill towards the stilling place and with speed, the shack was covered over with more bracken, and the pot, along with some containers, submerged into the plunge pool beneath the waterfall, where it was deepest, with only thin ropes linking the containers up to secured lines tied under shrub roots hanging into the water.

Soon the place was totally invisible, and the grain they brought with them was placed in a small cave, then covered with rocks and turf as best they could.

Donald thought of his plan again carefully, they could not stay in the bothy as Gillespie would have bought their location with coin, so they would be best to head down the hill towards Inversnaid again, with the purpose of hiding the pony in the woods whilst they took the boat north to the Ardlui Estate. Adam the factor there, being a friendly and fair man, and an old soldier too, would offer sanctuary and shelter. Gillespie would not dare cross the Ardlui Estate as they already knew of his reputation, and he knew of theirs.

As they finally approached the hiding place of the boat, Donald sent both lads to check carefully around the shoreline for trouble, but as they saw no one, or any sign of horses, they quickly returned to the boat to help their uncle prepare for launch. They loaded a few sacks of provisions along with a small cask of spirit as a gift to factor Adam for his kindness.

As the chatter from the excited lads grew louder, Donald had to shush them quiet for fear that their voices would travel too far across the silent Loch, and perhaps reveal their presence.

They pulled off from the shore, and Donald took to the oars for lack of wind, then they silently rowed out and into Loch Lomond seeking a breeze by which to hoist the sail and make progress onwards towards the Estate.

A dense loch mist clung to the water like a shroud, and the sail remained slack for want of a breeze.

The Loch was silent, still, and gloomy.

Some movement stirred out within the mist.

A boat, making fast towards them, with purpose and mission.

A 'requisitioned' skiff, with three men aboard came into view. Two redcoats rowing hard, and an officer seated at the bow, staring them down, with a loaded pistol ready in his hand.

"Ahoy there you rat," shouted Captain Gillespie, snorting in glee at the success of his calculation.

"I thought to find you here, and I have," he crowed, signalling for his soldiers to pull towards, and astern of Donald and the boys.

There was no way that Donald could out-row the skiff, as its keel was flat whilst his own boat had a deep draft to support the sail. He, and the boys were trapped out on the water well away from the safety of land.

As the larger skiff rapidly drew close, Gillespie levelled his gun as if to shoot Donald as soon as he had aim, and seeking to avert this crisis Donald released the oars, raised both hands high to show he was unarmed and nodded his head towards the barrel of spirit sticking up above the prow of his boat.

"What say you Sir, that you take this cask and it's worth, and spare my life for these childrens' sakes?" he implored across the narrow divide of water now between them.

"What say I shoot you dead, maggot, and take the cask along with these two pretty young vermin in your boat for my own sport and pleasure?" retorted the Captain.

Gillespie stood up now, for a better shot, and for a clearer view of his target, and he readied his gun cocking the flintlock slowly, closing one eye to steady his sights on Donald's head.

James cried out for mercy, trying to cover his uncle and protect him.

There was an explosion of powder, a blast of flame, and a sudden plume of sulphurous smoke as a shot went off, a pause, a brief seconds calm, as Gillespie dropped his pistol slightly and looked in confusion at the blood now seeping rapidly from the gaping wound in his chest.

He gasped, shuddering as the shock undid his balance, and the two soldiers behind him whimpered aloud as the skiff, pitched and lurched, as Gillespie staggered back into them.

He tried to raise his pistol towards Donald, but discharged his firearm too soon, sending his shot deep into the black water between them.

"But by god I am not ready for this, damn you!" he whimpered aloud turning back into the skiff and towards his men.

As if in slow motion the skiff unbalanced and capsized, and Gillespie sank swiftly into the oblivion of cold darkness beneath, his crew crying out for salvation as they could not swim.

They struggled, splashing, panicking, and thrashing, till their wet uniforms and attached weapons pulled them under the surface towards their silent and watery graves, leaving the skiff upended above as a fleeting memorial to their passing.

There was silence all around, Donald remained seated, and stunned, holding James close and shivering violently with the shock.

Behind them, at the back of the boat, Malcolm, at last released from his small hands, the still smoking and emptied pistol provided by farmer Smith, and then wept.

The mist remained close and silent, sheltering the crime, which was witnessed by none but Loch Lomond itself.

The Saga of Salty Wheels.

- an unexpected big adventure, following in Burts footsteps on the Worlds fastest Royal Enfield at Bonneville.

I am standing on the shady side of our large hire van, which is white in colour, to reflect as much of the intense Bonneville Salt Flats heat as possible. My racing leathers are white too, and although it is only eight o'clock in the morning, and still relatively cool for the location, I am dripping with sweat already.

The surging sense of panic has now departed after some deep breathing to calm my nerves, and I walk briskly over to the Royal Enfield engined, custom-build, two hundred and fifty c.c. turbo-pushrod motorcycle called 'Salty Wheels', climb aboard, and begin to methodically rev the throttle to keep the old brit iron alive.

We are on the famous long course of Speed Week, and the official waves me forward to where we are now on the start line of the course, staring ahead down the bi-coloured blur of white salt below and blue sky above, the distant Utah sandstone mountains a thread of beige blobs across the centre of my vision.

As the official gestures at me to proceed, my crew chief John slaps down the opened visor of my helmet, and my team push 'Salty Wheels' off the line to assist my start.

I twist the throttle, the bike catching and surging as it finds then delivers its modest power through the trembling engine to the back wheel and onto the compacted crispy salt which goes for miles and miles and miles.

I look forward into the surreal distance of the track, and I ask myself aloud "What the fuck!".

It was just a passing idea to help a local charity called the Joey Dunlop Foundation to raise some more money to support their facilities at Braddan House, a special needs residential centre on the Isle Of Man, home to the World famous T.T. motorcycle road races.

I settled in quite quickly after moving to the Island in 2010 to look after and care for my dear old mother.

At seventy five years old, a combination of the after-effects of Lymes disease, and the onset of dementia meant she could no longer support herself . . . she needed help.

I was suddenly faced with a stark choice, either she went into a nursing home, which would kill her due to the chemical constraints often placed on active people in those environments, or, I went and looked after her myself. A nursing home would cost £1000 a week, as she was deemed to have 'additional care needs' which costed additional money.

I did the sums. If I continued to work in Glasgow as an undertaker with the Co-operative Funeral Service, I would lose all my earnings paying for her care, and then go into debt to cover the remaining costs.

I took a deep breath and handed in my resignation.

To be honest, it was a relief to do so. After twenty-one years of employment things were steadily changing for the worse and I was better away from it all.

After selling my home and moving across to the Isle of Man, I took the opportunity to get a few miles done on my Triumph Thunderbird motorcycle around the quieter roads across the Island.

On one bright sunny day, I popped into the Joey Dunlop Foundation Centre at Braddan Bridge, to see the Manager, Kevin, a 'good egg' and a local worthy.

He was looking for fund-raising ideas, the committee was planning to build an extension to the Braddan House lodgings to create more specialist accommodation for guests.

He asked my opinion.

I suggested a limited bottling of whisky, as Joey Dunlop the famous T.T. racer ran a Bar in Ballymoney, Northern Ireland, and he was known to enjoy a drink or two of the amber nectar.

We discussed the practicalities of licensing, sourcing, and distribution.

I then headed back home to see how my dear old mother was doing, and to look into sourcing a whisky bottling from my numerous contacts in the industry.

Within the month, we had a good quality, high flavour malt blend which was primarily Glen Scotia, and was a lot better value and quality than some single malt options.

Over two thousand bottles were commissioned, transported to the Isle of Man, and put on sale in time for the annual T.T. road races of June 2013. Sales started well but declined as the poor weather drove bikers back home immediately the races finished.

To help boost awareness of the bottling, I suggested we got a few signed by racing stars, and auction them for publicity and funds.

Connor Cummins, a notable local racer, and John McGuinness, a big T.T. star, signed three of our bottles and they went into auction to raise money for the foundation.

The strategy worked well, so I elected to expand the theme, and asked Connor to sign a couple more bottles, which he was happy to do.

Later in the summer of 2013, I heard through the local news that an Island Team were going back to the Bonneville Salt Flats in Utah in 2014 to attend the centenary of Bonneville Speed Week.

The team had already set two consecutive records, exceeding 200 mph on a 500cc road bike in 2012 and they were keen to have another go. I liked the idea they represented and thought that a connection would be beneficial for the Joey Dunlop Foundation.

I arranged a meeting in the sea-side town of Laxey with representatives of the Team, who called themselves the Lonan Gentlemens Fellowship.

They were pleasant to talk to, and in need of funds for the 2014 visit, as costs of motorbike construction, logistics, and participation were high.

I offered to sell one of the bottles of Joey Whisky at a whisky auction. I signed and dated the bottle. The auctioned whisky raised a decent sum of money which I passed on to the Lonan Gentlemens Fellowship Fund.

The treasurer was impressed, especially when I explained more about how publicity and awareness could lead to more donations.

Before too long, I was asked if I would like to attend a committee meeting of the team and give a few ideas for consideration in relation to fund raising and publicity.

I offered some ideas, and they asked if I would like to join the team as a participant in the trip to Bonneville Speed Week 2014.

I immediately agreed, as a biker, fully aware of the legacy and iconic status of Speed Week.

I told my dear old mother that I would be going to Bonneville the following year to help a team try for some more land speed records. She seemed confused, but happy as I handed her another biscuit and cooling mug of tea.

As soon as she found the rest of the packet of biscuits on the kitchen table, they disappeared.

I discovered them six months later hidden under the toilet cistern in the bathroom, carefully wrapped in a plastic carrier bag.

The treasurer frequently complained about all the work she had to do unaided but refused to accept any help when it was offered.

I offered to help with a few tasks, but my main input was to organise two whisky tasting nights in a local bar. They both sold out, and a lot of money was raised. The team were delighted.

Things then began to get tense in the Lonan Gentlemens Fellowship, especially at committee meetings, as the big moment drew nearer to Bonneville Speed Week 2014, the Centenary year.

I didn't get involved in the growing conflict within the group.

I just stayed focused on what I needed to do to help once we got to the salt flats, so that the team could attempt more records.

A relative from Scotland offered to look after my mum whilst I was away in Utah. I provided her with flights, phone, car, food, and £100 cash a day for expenses.

The relative was delighted to get a paid free holiday, and at the end, asked for more cash.

My mum was oblivious to everything, spending her days walking up and down the local roads, with two electronic location devices attached to her so I knew where she was. The freedom and fresh air definitely helped her health and well-being despite her circumstances.

In August 2014, the Team, consisting of two hired vans, and eight people, arrived at the large, panoramic salt lake of Bonneville, only to find out through Facebook that the event had been cancelled the evening before due to unseasonal flooding across the course.

Everyone was gutted. We had come a long way and spent a lot of money in the process.

At that point, the atmosphere in the Team changed dramatically. The two vans became separate entities, effectively rival teams within the same group. The sudden toxicity shown by the treasurer towards the people in the van I was in was palpable.

Immediate return flights were considered, but deemed too expensive, so the van I was attached to headed back to Las Vegas where accommodation was cheaper. Once there, we devised an itinerary to make the most our time Stateside.

There were just four of us now, and I was glad of their company. It seemed obvious to me that they were the good guys.

We visited the Hoover Dam, the Grand Canyon, Red Rock Canyon, and all the other interesting places around Las Vegas.

Out of the blue, in the middle of Death Valley, California, Richard, the van driver and team captain announced that the team needed a second bike rider to honour the Fellowships pledge to its sponsors. He then went on to ask if I would like to ride in Speed Week 2016, which was when they expected to return, if the salt was dry, and not flooded again.

I didn't hesitate, I had seen the salt now. I sensed the big adventure. . . . I said yes.

Back on the Isle of Man, I met up with the gang and suggestions were made for a suitable size and style of bike for me. It was decided that it should be a special build. A 250cc methanol-fuelled pushrod. These engines were old, rare and difficult to get right, but with the experience in the team, it was do-able.

The other half of the Lonan Gentlemens Fellowship were not being communicative, and there were concerns that funds raised were not getting distributed to the Team as a whole.

The Police ended up being involved, and after a very prolonged enquiry, the Police investigation resulted in charges being brought against the Treasurer and her partner for the theft of significant amounts of Fellowship funds, money donated by the locals on the Island, and by the wider biking community. The lengthy trial by jury that ensued, ended in a conviction and jail time for the pair.

I kept my dear old mum informed about what was going on within the Team, but she no longer had the facility to understand. An alteration had come over her due, I suspected, to the toxic and damaging dementia medication she has recently been prescribed . . . in good faith, by her doctor. When she responded to my question as to why she had been so sad over the past few weeks with the statement that she just wanted to 'throw herself away', I was then certain that her new medication was having a detrimental effect. Despite the dementia, she had always been happy and content within her little shrinking world but not anymore and I was shocked. It was not what I would have expected from her and at that point I became much more aware of how toxic pharmaceuticals can be. I decided that if I wanted to live longer, I should avoid a doctors' surgery, and, more importantly, big Pharma products as much as possible.

Over the following week, I steadily stepped down her drug consumption, and she returned to her old self. Cheery and positive, walking happily up and down the local, quiet country road which she never tired of. The fresh air and exercise doing her good.

I never let her be subjected to prescription medication again. She got proper nutrition and a few herbal supplements. They did a great job, especially the devils claw herbal capsules for her arthritis and the smoothies made from fresh fruit for the vitamin and fibre.

Every Wednesday I helped to build the bike that would take me down the salt in 2016.

The frame was built by the team captain Richard. It was light, old-school, and beautifully welded to hold an option of three Royal Enfield 250cc Continental GT pushrod engines, one of which was donated by a local museum, another bought from an old biker, and a third, bought at the Stafford Motorcycle Show in England as a working GT motorcycle from which I was loaned the engine, temporarily.

I tried my level best to do some fabrication and engineering, but my skills were non-existent.

I'm just crap at mechanical stuff.

Being rubbish as a mechanic I volunteered to do the administration and forms for the Team instead, and they agreed.

The other chaps in the Team got on with it. Putting together, over time, a splendid, characterful wee motorcycle which really looked the part for a run or two down the salt.

I doubted I would ever get a record as I was no racer and the small bike was fragile.

Just being able to say I had been 'down the salt' at Bonneville would be enough.

I bought a D.V.D. of 'The World's Fastest Indian' with Anthony Hopkins playing the part of Burt Munro, a stubborn character made famous by his determination to race his Indian Scout modified motorcycle at the salt flats back in the 1960's.

We sat down one night to watch it, so that my mother could see what I would be doing the following year.

I thought it was a great film, and wonderful to see the event from a non-Hollywood cinematic viewpoint.

I asked my dear old mum if she had enjoyed the film. She said nothing but seemed happy. She was talking a lot less now, the sun slowly and steadily setting on her outside world.

I held her hand and gave her a hug, and then made her another cup of tea, with a biscuit too.

The bike soon took shape as bits and pieces were added to the rolling chassis.

Richard suggested he would be co-ordinator, whilst John would be my crew chief on the salt, supervising tickets, times, and places, making sure I was where I needed to be.

John was rock-steady, a retired fire fighter with over 40 years service, 20 of them as a senior fire and rescue officer. He was affable, stoic, and with experience helping on the salt.

Although in his seventies, he was youthful in his outlook, easy-going, and focussed on the mission.

I was glad to have him in my Team.

Richard was chilled, resourceful and an athletic man in his 50's. He builds great bikes from scratch.

A lifetime grass-tracker, and Isle Of Man sprint champion, he was the one who set a consecutive Record on the salt in 2012 on his 500cc motorbike, exceeding 200mph, and getting a bright red cap to honour his admission to the '200mph Club'.

He is a man who has been well weathered by the passing of the years, lean, tough, enthusiastic, decent, and dependable. He is simply a good man to know, and to have around in any situation.

My mum frowned briefly over her mug of tea one day and asked if she could go to see the bikes at Bonneville. I explained that it will be very hot, that the tea was not very good there, and that they have no biscuits. She soon changed her mind and asked for extra biscuits while I was away on the mission instead, to which I agreed.

The local cottage hospital agreed to look after her whilst I was away.

Confined to her bed now, it was easier for me to get prepared for the forthcoming challenge.

It happened suddenly, she walked out to the garden gate, paused, thought slowly, and with difficulty, then wandered back into the house, and climbed the stairs to her bedroom.

She sat down on her bed, looked out the window for a while, sipping the fresh-made tea I had brought up for her, then decided she would just go to bed, and stay there instead.

She was safe, cosy, comfortable. The outside world of country roads and green fields was no longer for her.

She stayed in bed for the next three years.

It made looking after her a lot easier. I could relax a bit, knowing she was fine, happy in her new reality, with no worries or concerns about outside threats.

The bike was nearing completion. The guys had done a fantastic job with the aesthetics and functionality, and it had only cost me £8,000 so far, what with components, spares, batteries and all the stuff needed, including electric starter rollers.

As soon as it was ready, we loaded the bike into my van and headed to a remote place to test it.

It was a complete disaster.

I blame that fact that it had been set up to run on methanol fuel, and that the engine simply could not take it.

Three of us pushed, cajoled, and tried to bump start the machine on the electric rollers I had bought on e-bay.

No luck, so we re-configured the carburettor and tried again. It nearly started.

We tried again. Same routine, then the bike started with a coughing splutter, then a roar.

Richard, who was more experienced, donned a helmet, and jumped onto the bike, and headed off down the road.

The engine sounded good, raspy and powerful,

Then the engine went silent and died. The bike rolled to a halt.

Richard started to push the bike back towards us as we ran down the road to meet him, to see what had gone wrong.

We discovered, after some exploration, that the piston had blown. A neat cut of molten metal where the heat of the methanol on the spark plug had caused the 700 degrees heat generated, to melt the aluminium clean through near the centre of the piston.

We loaded the damaged creature back into the van and headed off home. I immediately ordered three new pistons from the Royal Enfield accessory supplier.

The following week we headed back to the same spot to try again, and within minutes we got the same result, . . . another blown piston.

The pistons cost £60 each, the equivalent of a decent bottle of malt whisky, so I was not too happy when a total of five pistons were popped over the next six weeks of testing.

The project is turning into a disaster.

But the bike looked great.

My old mum went down with a virus about then, which made her cough a lot. At times, being bed-bound, she started to choke whilst coughing, so I sat with her, holding her hand and comforting her with cough syrup and fresh brewed tea fed through a baby bottle.

After a few days, she rallied round again, and I could return my attention to the bike, the mission, and to Bonneville Speed Week 2016.

A member of the Vintage Motorcycle Club on the Island suddenly found time on his hands due to a cancelled holiday, and declared his interest in joining the Team for the adventure. As he had decades of professional experience running a motorcycle dealership in Douglas, the Islands capital we decided to invite him to join us for a meeting.

Ritchy popped round one evening to see what it was all about, and we clicked immediately. He really knew his stuff and it showed.

He was a grey-bearded, mature man, academic-looking and patient, with a time-served instinct for old British motorbikes.

He talked about his shop in Douglas, and his experience working on old British bikes, especially those ridden by notable T.T. racers like Mike Hailwood.

I reckoned that if Ritchy was good enough for a road racing hero like Hailwood, then I would be very lucky to have him on our Team.

After agreeing to join us, he immediately suggested that the fuel be changed from methanol to petrol.

Others were reluctant to agree, but had to acknowledge his experience, and soon the engine was running hard, powerful, and fast, proving that he was right in his assessment. I had no more blown pistons after the change from methanol to petrol.

Back in my bike shed, the popped pistons, buckled valves, and some freshly bent push-rods were lined up on a shelf above the door and a message written in black felt-tip pen underneath, 'Sacrifices o the God of speed'. It's what Burt Munro did in his shed, so I did it too in mine, after all, it might help a little, and it looked good.

The bike was nearly complete, but the second engine, built by another Bonneville racer needed major work done to it. This second engine was the special-build turbo-powered version and the modern Mitsubishi turbo was over-blowing unburnt fuel right out the exhaust.

A local amateur turbo-specialist was approached for help, and agreed to knock the engine into shape.

Along with Richard, the turbo expert known as 'the Doc', spent five days cutting, trimming, fettling and tuning the 250cc turbo pushrod into a fine-balanced work of art and pure function.

The Doc transformed the engine into something incredible.

Such was the unexpected success of this turbo engine, that Richard decided, along with the rest of the Team, that it should be first option for the salt, so I had to change classes on the entry forms submitted months earlier to the Southern California Timing Association, the custodians of Bonneville Speed Week.

The Timing Association were very helpful and friendly, unlike some other U.S. bureaucratic departments I had to contact. As I needed an Environmental Protection Agency licence to import my bike into the U.S. I had to approach the relevant licensing authorities, and after delays, they eventually directed me to a bureaucrat who made my life hell as best he could.

Obstructive, arrogant, uncommunicative, and blunt, it was clear that the bitter man I had to deal with relished exercising the power that he had. I had to play a very tactful and patient game till finally, at the last minute, I received the licence I needed.

Without it, I would not be able to participate in the event.

I needed racing insurance too, and this proved very difficult to pin down but, eventually I got cover.

After this, the logistics of packaging the bike and its extras into an aluminium-clad steel crate for transport was a simple task.

A plane was booked to take the bike out to the U.S. as it turned out to be not only a lot quicker to do than shipping on a container boat, but also cheaper, due to global fuel-cost prices in relation to trade.

Vans were hired in Los Angeles, Visas were applied for, and a carnet 'Inventory of container content' was prepared to accompany the bike and bits.

It proved complicated and expensive.

The costs had soared to £16,000 for my mission and we had still to pay for planes and hotel rooms. Bonneville Speed Week was not for the faint-heated or financially squeamish.

Just before I left, I lifted my dear old mum out of her bed and carried her slowly down the stairs, out into the fresh light of day, and placed her carefully into the car. I drove to the local cottage hospital and trundled her in one of their available wheelchairs to an open ward, where a friendly nurse met us and introduced herself to my mum. The ward would be her home for the two weeks I was away. I kissed her goodbye. She sat in a hospital chair, oblivious to her surroundings, silent and detached in her inner world.

I felt a pang of guilt, but as I had cared for her on my own for six years, I think I had earned the break.

Not, that it would be particularly relaxing.

The Team finally make it without incident to Las Vegas, our intermediary stop before Wendover, and a chance to acclimatise to the heat of the roasting Nevada sun. It really was hot. Sunscreen was slapped on twice a day, extra water was drunk, and we spent an afternoon gaping at the obese citizens strolling up and down the surreal environment of the Vegas Strip. Las Vegas was fine for a visit, but anyone with sense will soon want to leave this glitter-town, so, having collected the hired van, then the bike crate from Los Angeles, which was a total nightmare to navigate, we headed up the open desert road from Las Vegas to Wendover for Speed Week.

As soon as we had left Las Vegas, with Richard driving at the wheel, we relaxed a little and fell silent within the endless stark and broken beauty of the landscape around us. John and Richy were deep in thought for a while as we took in the barren, dust strewn sparseness of the rolling Nevada desert.

It was so very different from home, and we could imagine the old wild west playing out amongst the rocks, boulders and tuffs of driftwood all around us.

Heading northwards up Highway 93 it took us six hours of steady cruising until we finally arrived at our destination, Wendover, hub of Bonneville, a distinctive one-road highway town of 1,400 living souls.

When we arrived, it was already busy and bustling with petrol-heads and speed-chasers.

Our accommodation was the basic, but comfortable Wendover Nugget Hotel and Casino, a simple, unglamorous venue, which had air conditioning that worked.

We headed firstly to West Wendover Fire Station to say hello to friends from previous visits, and to check that it was ok to use a corner of the fire station as our off-salt base for running repairs and access to tools. As before, the fire Chief was hospitable and generous, and we unpacked my crate in the carpark at the back of the Station, then headed down to the salt just as the evening sun began to sink golden and shimmering across the crisp white salt.

The moment that we arrived on the salt was emotional, as we stared over a surreal and other-worldly place, so very alien to our senses, but still, a familiar and friendly alien as most of us had been here before.

Tomorrow was the beginning of Speed Week, and we smelled the air which was full of heat and excitement, opportunity, and risk.

Far in the distance, I thought that I could make out the ghost of Burt Munro driving his battered old car and towing an Indian scout streamliner motorcycle, and everything suddenly felt a bit timeless.

We were all in the van keeping as cool as possible, queued up on the short course, waiting patiently for me to take my virgin run on the salt, and to see if we could actually do it.

I have named my bike 'Salty Wheels' which I think is a damn fine name, not too pretentious, sentimental or boring, just right.

As soon as the bike was rolled out of the van and onto the salt surface, the tyres coated with a film of creamy, crisp salt, baptising my bike to his purpose, and bonding him to his name.

My first run down the salt was a residual confusing blur, but successful and we complete our 'qualifying run' with ease.

As salty wheels and I left the start line, I felt the euphoric thrill of it all. We were here, and it was happening, here, right now, and for real.

The following day, Monday was the first day of racing, officially.

All vehicles had completed their 'test' run under speed limitations to ensure that both vehicle and driver were fit to participate.

The salt was awash with custom cars, trucks, hot-rods, motorcycles, streamliners, and an eclectic assortment of hybrid things on wheels. The sight of them all was unique, surreal, exotic, and thereafter amplified by the array of human characters in and around the vehicles, and then there was the salt flat itself, cradling the event within its elemental embrace.

Salty Wheels and I headed down the salt, and after about a mile, Salty spluttered, coughed and the engine died, then I had to pull off the track towards the support vehicle road.

Back at the Wendover fire station, Richard, Ritchy and John surrounded the bike and analysed the problem. Within the hour, it was recognised as a carbonation issue, and it got sorted.

The following day, Tuesday, 'Salty' and I headed off the line of the short course, gathering pace and with the engine pulling strong and sweet. Momentum built and so did the speed, faster, and faster, until just before the second mile marker, there was a bang from the engine, and the bike swiftly decelerated. On stopping at the support vehicle lane, I looked down to see the chain had snapped.

Later, we found that the woodruff key was sheared, and that there was a bolt missing from the internal casing.

We had set a record, but to confirm the record, we need to 'back it up' with another run the next day.

The next day, Wednesday, the gear change jammed in third, and I missed finding fourth gear, so, the record was lost.

It is just the way it goes.

The team worked late into the night at the fire station, cutting, grinding, adapting, and fitting the third, spare engine into the bike frame. I tried to help, but I was only getting in the way.

The next day, Thursday, the short course was now closed, and we move to the middle course where 'Salty' and I head off down the course, accelerating slowly, so slowly towards another record.

We set a record time, a low one, but enough to qualify for another back-up run.

Now, after another period in impound, we had one day left to back it up and consolidate the record for the class of machine. My team worked relentlessly all afternoon to get the engine working its best, defying the intense heat and uncomfortable environment within the impound stockade.

I headed off to buy them all shaved-ice flavoured cones from a small vendor close by. It's the least I could do under the circumstances.

It was Friday, last day of Speed Week, and I had not slept well, only about two hours in fact, and I felt shattered.

Salty Wheels was ready to go, we both felt the excitement intensely. Richard, Richy and John remained cool and calm, because that's the type of people they are. It is just before 8a.m.

Richard takes the time to remind me that any record I achieve may not seem that much in terms of modern car speeds, but at Bonneville, a record, is a record, is a record, so there!

If anyone could do it, everyone would, but they don't, because they can't.

I am reassured.

We were now on the famous long course of Speed Week, and the official waved me forward to where I was now on the start line of the eleven mile course, staring ahead down the bi-coloured blur of white salt below and blue sky above, the distant Utah sandstone mountains a thread of beige blobs across the centre of my vision.

As he waved me to proceed, my crew chief John slaps down the opened visor of my helmet, and my team push 'Salty Wheels' off the line to assist my start.

I twist the throttle, the bike catching and surging as it finds, then delivers its modest power through the trembling engine to the back wheel and onto the compacted crispy salt which goes for miles and miles and miles.

I look forwards and into the surreal distance of the track, and I ask myself "What the fuck!"

We gather pace, and 'Salty' feels the moment, taking the pace forwards, faster, and faster and onwards whilst I hang on, tucking deeper towards the heart of the beautiful machine, and we are now as one, and going faster and faster.

As we cross the final timing line at the two mile mark, I raise my head up and ease off the throttle, but let us both continue onwards for quarter of a mile down the track, as this is our last time, our last opportunity, out last moment to connect with Bonneville.

'Salty' rumbles forwards and I embrace the shimmering entity that is the salt.

We eventually stop by the support track and wait for my Team in the van to arrive.

For a few minutes, all is as one, all is peaceful, all is sublime, Salty and I can hear the universe breathing.

I carried the tatty cardboard box, just delivered by the postman, up the stairs to my mum's bedroom.

She was motionless, but comfortable as I ripped the cardboard off the package, and removed the shining, heavy prize.

I showed her the trophy and read what it said out loud to her.

BONNEVILLE SPEED WEEK
BONNEVILLE NATIONALS
2016 AUGUST 13th - 19th
129b
Salty Wheels
250cc/APS-PBG
74.729 mph

She remained blank and distant, so I asked her if she wanted some warm tea and a mushy biscuit in her feeding bottle.

She smiled, and blinked that she did.

That night, I closed the curtains, light the fire, and poured some beer and then some whisky as I settled down with the trophy beside the television and re-watched the D.V.D. of 'The World's Fastest Indian" with Anthony Hopkins playing the role of Burt Munro.

As the drama unfolded on the screen, I got drunk, slowly, softly, and when the film ended I got up and went to the room next door to give 'Salty Wheels' a hug, and say thank-you to the bike for the journey we made together and for the big adventure we shared at Bonneville.

Water Horse Distillery.

- How dreams can come true, except that nightmares are dreams too, and we should never forget that.

August 2017

The two pals meet in a local pub called the Ben Nevis, situated on the corner of Argyle Street and Corunna Street in a fashionable, bohemian part of Glasgows west end.

Corry is an eccentric young man with mousy-brown hair, thin, tall, and slightly fragile, who gets rather intense a lot of the time, especially over the subject of good quality whisky and other liquors.

Cammy is shorter, stocky, with gingery hair and a mature, matching beard, with a natural affinity for cheap, practical clothing usually sourced from local charity shops. He has an easy going way about him and likes attention to detail.

Both are mildly autistic, intelligent, and share a passion for certain specifics in life, including death metal music and distilling.

Cammy is at Heriot-Watt University in Edinburgh and is about to graduate with impressive results in his final exams.

Corry, on the other hand, could never afford university, and being dyslexic, has avoided the traumas of studying and exams, so instead, works at a small brewery, specialising in low volume bottled craft beers and lagers. This is what he is good at and it's what he wants to do in life.

Corry is drinking a pint of I.P.A. with a Glencairn of Bunnahabhain 12yo, whilst Cammy, feeling the need to celebrate, has a pint of milk stout along with a Springbank 12yo at cask strength.

All is good, the bar is busy, and the folk band have not arrived yet to disrupt the conversations with loud live music.

They talk about this, then that, and then, as the conversation grows more intense, about how they will start up their own little distillery, somewhere local, and make it different from the usual, a hub, a venue, a special 'experience'.

September 2017

Cammy phones Corry for a meet-up and complains about the lack of job opportunities in the scotch whisky industry if you want to do something creative and hands-on. There are plenty of opportunities in marketing, and on-trade sales too, but it's not what he wants to spend the rest of his life doing.

November 2017

The two pals go to Glasgow's Whisky Festival, taking place at Hampden Park Football Stadium, which is handy for the train afterwards. They have afternoon tickets so as to get to the venue when it's a bit cooler and to try the best malts before the bottles get emptied. They take notebooks for jottings, and make sure to chat civilly to the distillery staff behind the tables holding assortments of bottled malt-treats.

It's a good event. Not too crowded. Not too expensive, and plenty of smaller companies are represented at the tables, which provides diversity of tasting opportunities and conversations.

They meet a middle-aged, greying, affable man called Prentis Dick at the Deanston table, and soon get chatting.

Prentis is a self-made man. He has been lucky over the years in pulling himself up by the boot straps, starting off as a labourer in the 1970's, completing a traditional building trade apprenticeship while it was still possible to do such a thing, and then shortly thereafter, starting his own building and maintenance company 'P. Dick Builders Ltd:'

Specialising in long-term maintenance contracts with local government, and the acquisition of small building plots in urban areas known as brown field sites, he has made a good living for himself over the last few decades and is able to take his lovely wife Sheryl, and only daughter Aimee, on luxury cruises, and frequent long-weekend shopping trips to New York.

Life is good when you have a few million in the bank, although some of his house-buyers are threatening to sue the Company due to structural faults in his new-build homes. There are also problems with chemical seepage killing the grass lawns, freshly-installed into the tiny gardens, and some consultant employed by the home owners claims that chemical analysis shows there to be arsenic salts in the soil with could be harmful to people over the long term, but what do you expect from the re-commissioning of industrial urban land. His friends in the local council will keep that problem at bay, after all, he has paid them plenty to do so.

Prentis is balding and bespectacled, but he looks after himself in the gym and takes no shit from anyone. He has never lost touch with his roots and calls a spade a spade.

The three men are chatting amicably by the Deanston table, when something seems to happen out of thin air. Cammy says he's a qualified distiller, Corry works in a brewery, and Prentis is looking to sink an investment into something to do with whisky, which he has always had a passion for.

A self-made man does not store money in the bank. Banks take money, they don't give it.

Prentis suddenly asks the two lads if they are interested in helping with his project, to build a distillery.

Corry and Cammy are interested.

December 2017

Corry, Cammy and Prentis meet in the Ben Nevis Bar on a quiet Tuesday night, all three have pens and paper. Cammy has a calculator.

All in, the starting capital needs to be several million pounds for premises, stills, administrative formalities, wages, licences, malted barley, casks, electricity, bottling facilities and an office.

The two lads seem phased by the amount, but Prentis is confident, and sees the opportunity to remove all his wealth from his building company, P. Dick Builders Ltd closing it down and transferring assets into P. D. Distillers Ltd.

Should any homebuyer successfully sue over the houses he built, they will get nothing in the form of compensation if P. Dick Ltd: no longer exists. He does not disclose his thoughts to the two lads.

January 2018

The contracts have been signed, and P. D. Distillers Ltd: is looking for premises as Prentis has now decided that Finnieston is too expensive, even though the two lads prefer the area for its potential.

A Unit is found at number 13, Castings Court, Middlefield Industrial Estate, Falkirk, which Prentis quickly agrees to accept as it comes with local government support and is rent-free for the first year. It has five thousand square feet of utility space and only costs £20,000 a year to rent . . . after the first year.

The local council like to support fledgling, innovative enterprises with vision and passion.

Licences are quickly secured and refurbishment is swift due to Prentis's building connections.

Forsyths the, Scottish-based, copper pot still fabricators, provide a quote for the supply and installation of two modest stills. Prentis is shocked at the outrageous price and immediately buys two new, two thousand litre capacity Holstein stills from China which are cheaper.

Cammy and Corry are not sure, but they're contracted into the business now as junior partners, so go with the decision.

Prentis explains that these types of stills can make great whisky and also make gin and vodka to supplement income until the whisky is ready to sell.

Corry and Cammy are now working fourteen-hour days, whilst Prentis is getting a bit stressed with the cash-flow.

Prentis decides to call the distillery 'Water Horse Distillery' as his daughter Aimee, who likes Kelpies, thinks it would be really, really lovely. He loves the name too, as his daughter made it up, and he can patent it, and get the social media addresses too,

. . . and it sounds much better than 'Dick Distillery Ltd:' which was his original choice.

March 2018

The day of opening has arrived, and despite the hastily installed equipment still giving problems.

The three entrepreneurs agree to stick with rectifying bought-in ethanol from alcohols.co.uk and to pass it through the Holsteins along with botanicals bought mainly from e-bay, with some picked from a local public green space called Dollar Park, which means they can claim they are using local ingredients.

Thanks to Cammys calculations and to Corrys blending instincts, the resulting gin is rather decent.

Cammy decides to bottle at 43% vol and Corry selects an appropriate bottle design and creates a label.

'Water Horse Gin' is well received, and the first sales are made on the opening day, attended by local worthies, trade mixologists, and 'influencers' from the internet.

Prentis dresses up as a Water Horse for the occasion, managing the press release and supervising internet content for Instagram, Twitter, and Facebook.

Aimee buys a new dress and looks lovely for photos on Facebook and Instagram.

Everyone agrees that they are off to a good start.

April 2018

Aimee has left school and hates her beautician course at the local college. Prentis offers her the job of Media and Out-Reach Executive at Water Horse Distillery as she is good with people, and enthusiastic too.

Corry and Cammy are not happy to discover that she is getting paid £40,000 a year plus bonus whilst they remain on minimum wage, plus a small, junior partners annual productivity dividend as determined by Prentis.

Aimee is, small, blond, slim, fussy, and neurotic about her health, and that of her pet dog Weebeeny, a pedigree poodle who has regular bloating problems and is rather nervous most of the time.

When Aimee is in a good mood, everything is fine, but she will get very moody very quickly if required to help in the distillery. Aimee thinks that work is for workers. She is an Executive, and very busy reaching out to consumers.

May 2018

Consolidating sales on the publics initial gin enthusiasm has not gone to plan. The distributors are fed up with Aimee's constant interference, so Prentis sacks them, employing a new distributor with a more prestigious portfolio of top-brands. It costs a lot more, but they are now getting Water Horse Gin into more prestigious retailers and bars, especially in London.

Everyone is delighted when Harrods begin stocking their gin.

Prentis increases the prices across the gin range by £5.

Aimee sells toy water horses to all her friends on Facebook at cost price.

Aimee goes to London for a promotional party but flies back early the following day as she misses Weebeeny. The party was a good one, and she met some lovely people, and has got an invitation for herself along with mummy and daddy to go to the Henley Royal Regatta in a few weeks to meet some well-connected people who may be useful to know.

June 2018

Corry and Cammy experiment with rum and whisky styles, as demand has dropped for their gin. Nobody seems interested in their vodka, 'Water Horse Vodka' - 'a splash of otherworld fantasy'.

They think that Prentis has priced it too high at £50 a bottle.

The two lads decide to arrange a Kickstarter funding based on rum and whisky futures.

Prentis agrees as he is concerned about the cost of oak barrels now that his young team are producing 'brown spirits', as he likes to call them.

Prentis, his wife Sheryl, and Aimee have gone to Henley Royal Regatta at Henley-on-Thames, where hotel rooms are extortionately expensive.

They have a wonderful time, and Aimee is happy she could take Weebeeny to hold and cuddle although the boat races are very boring, and the Australian team beat the Romanian team, so, who cares anyway.

Their hosts, the Distribution company, hold a marquee drinks party, which their guests are delighted to attend as the weather is cool and it looks like rain.

Here, Prentis is introduced to Piers Bally-Winser, a hospitality entrepreneur and 'Imagineer'

Piers is charming, polite, humorous, flattering and laughs a lot.

Standing six feet tall, he is from top to toe, a carelessly dressed, dishevelled home-counties toff who is quick to discreetly drop into the conversation that Eton and Oxbridge are his alma maters.

Prentis is impressed.

Back in the hotel room, Sheryl confides to Prentis that she thinks that Piers is a 'pompous big arsehole' and warns Prentis not to have anything further to do with him.

Aimee thinks he's 'cute'.

July 2018

The Kickstarter project has been a huge success, and subscriptions for limited edition 'futures' has experienced so much demand that Prentis decides to extend the limits of the editions considerably to meet public interest. £600,000 is finally raised. Cammy and Corry are delighted, although they had originally only targeted raising half that amount and feel that Prentis has plundered goodwill.

The two lads deal with all the paperwork to make sure that customers are looked after.

With the money in, they persuade Prentis to buy a couple of alembic stills from Portugal, both with 2,500 litres capacity, and then arrange for the brewery up the road to supply their required ferment.

They start producing a range of flavoursome whisky along with some molasses rum, and increase their working days to sixteen hours to manage the new warehouse unit recently commissioned across the car park.

They both feel tired from the physically hard work of their new duties. They will more time off at Christmas.

August 2018

Piers Bally-Winser arrives for a visit, and to interview Prentis along with Aimee for a lifestyle magazine. The interview goes very well, and Piers learns a lot about Prentis and his adoration for his only daughter.

Aimee gushes and blushes throughout the interview and is responsive to Piers subtle seductions. Weebeeny won't stop barking and has to be locked in the Range Rover with the windows open a bit for air.

September 2018

Piers returns for a second visit and takes Prentis out for a private lunch. He asks Prentis if he has considered lobbying the London parliament for better support for small craft, artisan distillers.

Prentis is very taken with the idea, although he's not actually sure if it is necessary and whether the cost justifies the possible results.

Corry has to go home as he is sick. Cammy loses his temper and threatens to walk out if he does not get some help.

Prentis phones a friend to arrange a labourer to help at the Distillery, for a few days.

Aimee takes Weebeeny for a walk in the car park, but when Weebeeny throws up, Aimee has to take her pet home for aromatherapy.

Prentis terminates Corry and Cammys' productivity bonus and Junior partner status, which was never fixed in their employment contract anyway, and stops them spending so much money on casks when he can get them a lot cheaper from a speyside cooperage.

October 2018

Piers visits Water Horse Distillery again and persuades Prentis that if he pays £50,000 to a lobby company, he will get to meet the Minister of Agriculture and Fisheries in Westminster.

The meeting will be about an hour, but no more, and it could put Prentis in contention for a possible O.B.E. or M.B.E. depending on how the Queen is advised.

This opportunity would, of course, require a further commitment of £100,000 in donation by Prentis to a political party.

Prentis thinks it would be a bit much, but is persuaded by his wife Sheryl, and Aimee, that he deserves it as proper recognition for what he's done for the community, so he should pay the money, and perhaps give a bit more to a political party, just to secure the honour.

Piers advises that it does not matter which political party he chooses to give a donation to, as they are all the same anyway, and just do what they are told by the banks.

November 2018

Prentis decides to bottle and ship all the gin and rum futures to Kickstarter backers.

Corry and Cammy complain that the maturing casks are nowhere near ready yet, and that Bruichladdich made that same mistake a few years ago which pissed off some loyal customers with overly-young raw, immature peated whisky.

They say that the casks should be left another three years, however Prentis proceeds to bottle and ship all the futures cases, and Kickstarter backers then complain, feeling short-changed. Some aggrieved backers take to social media and chat-groups, so Prentis decides to bottle a special collectable edition of some re-casked, bought-in whisky, which is in fact tastes very mature for its young age thanks to the 'finishing' use of expensive, good quality, small casks imported directly from Hungary by Corry.

It is expensively packaged and sells out instantly. Piers suggests putting one bottle into an auction house, where his pals in London will bump up the bids on his instruction to ensure the bottle sells for three times the expected price. It works, the publicity is enormous, and bottlers and collectors are now phoning the Distillery daily to try and buy a cask for themselves as an investment.

Prentis hires Piers as a consultant on £50,000 a year retainer, plus bonuses.

December 2018

Prentis launches the 'Three Mystical Peaks' landscape collectable edition of Water Horse Distillery.

A bottle of rum, whisky and gin, all in one wooden boxed package, imported at short notice from China for very little money. The fans love it. It's so Celtic and rustic and traditional.

Corry and Cammy are a lot quieter now, keeping out the way and avoiding communicating with Prentis, which suits him fine.

Weebeeny is sick again.

When Aimee takes the poodle to the vets, the nasty lady vet explains that dogs are not supposed to be vegan, and that Aimees care for her dog is abusive.

Aimee is so upset that she cannot drive her car, so Prentis has to uplift her, and after hearing the story, considers suing the vet.

Piers is phoned and recommends only paying the vet only five percent of her fees, and as such, by law it will be considered bad debt, and not default.

Prentis and Aimee like the idea.

April 2019

Piers advises Prentis that the Liberal Party office in Westminster is delighted to be in receipt of £150,000 as a donation from an innovative, dynamic, and enterprising progressive Company with vision, dynamism, and green social ethics.

The full amount donated is sourced from a bank business loan based on the collateral of stock the distillery has in maturing casks.

Piers discreetly advises that Prentis will have to wait at least eighteen months before he can potentially receive an invitation from her Majesty for recipiency of an O.B.E.

To get things rolling, Piers suggests diversifying the range of branded products, including T-shirts, woolly hats, stuffed toys, and tins of shortbread, all with the Water Horse logo and brand colouring.

Prentis agrees, and leases a shop in Falkirk to act as the outlet for the branded goods.

Business starts slowly, but as soon as tourist season arrives in May, and with visitors flocking in to see the Falkirk Wheel along the road, sales pick up.

All the branded goods are made in China but sold under the trade marked brand 'Water Horse Distillery of Scotland' to confuse the customers into thinking that the goods are local.

The stunt works.

Prentis and Piers meet civil servants from the Department of Agriculture and Fisheries at Whitehall however, the meeting seems cold and uninformative, and possibly a waste of time.

It only lasts forty-five minutes, during which time Piers does most of the talking.

The civil servants seem bored.

May 2019

Piers advises Prentis to continue leasing the distillery building, and to cut down on operational costs. He also suggests that Corry and Cammy be re-contracted as self-employed so as to make the minimum wage they receive look like a 'living wage' on the books.

Prentis agrees.

Piers advises that Prentis sell all the existing stocks of casks to another Company PiersPrentis Group Ltd: which will act as an independent bottler for all official bottlings.

Prentis agrees when Piers suggests that, like Karuizawa in Japan, if there are no distillery bottlings available, then any alternative is 'investment grade stock', and worth double the money to collectors and the 'brand faithful'.

June 2019

Piersprentis Group Ltd launches quietly, with no publicity.

Only Piers and Prentis are aware of its existence.

August 2019

Piers suggests that they buy out a local pub which is on the point of closure.

It is centrally located, full of Victorian period fixtures and fittings, and the old man who owns it is now an alcoholic, so wants to sell.

Piers negotiates with the old man to buy his pub, after giving him a lot to drink, and then offers shares in PiersPrentis Ltd: instead of cash payment, and this is accepted.

The old man sells for £150,000 of shares, and Piers immediately closes the pub, stripping out the period interior and selling everything for £200,000 to a friend behind a new retro-style bar opening in Soho, London.

He orders the now empty shell of the pub to be completely refurbished as a wine emporium, delicatessen, and coffee shop, employing two young Romanian women to run it.

The shopfitters have to sue to get paid.

They only get 50% of what they are due. . . eventually.

After two months, he sells the business without Prentiss' knowledge, and pockets £350,000.

Stocks of casks from Water Horse Distillery now belonging to PiersPrentis Ltd are re-valued at four times their previous value as they are considered 'investment grade' stock, and 'aspirational'.

September 2019

Piers doubles the annual rental charge to Water Horse Distillery for the storing of casks belonging to PiersPrentis Ltd.

Prentis agrees, as its for tax reasons.

Piers suggests that he should get an increase in annual dividend of £50,000 as he is the primary consultant to the distillery.

Prentis agrees.

Piers suggests that Prentis charge the Distillery as an independent consultant, for £5,000, as it will enhance his personal career portfolio.

Prentis agrees.

December 2019

Sales are poor for the time of year, and Corry and Cammy complain that prices for the products are too high.

Awkward questions are asked about Piers exact involvement with Water Horse Distillery.

Prentis refuses to comment and puts his two distillers on a zero-hour contracts to prevent any further insubordination.

Piers suggests an innovation called 'Investors Club' where selected customers are offered futures in the best 10% of casks in Inventory. Invitation only, and very exclusive, the invited customer will pay £20,000 for a cask, which will sell for an estimated £40,000 in about four years at auction. The proposed hammer price being assured by the Distillery itself on behalf of PiersPrentis Ltd, should casks fail to achieve the expected hammer price.

December 24th 2019

Corry and Cammy suddenly walk out of Water Horse Distillery on the Friday before Christmas and never return.

Aimee gets Weebeeny a Santa clause costume for Christmas.

Prentis buys Aimee a designer T-shirt costing £1,000 for her Christmas.

January 2020

Prentis employs five Polish migrant workers to run Water Horse Distillery.

March 2020

Sales are poor, and fans seem to be getting bored of the brand.

Online 'influencers' are talking about other distilleries now, despite Prentis sending them miniatures through the post and inviting them to a 'WaterhorseFest Open Day' with plastic bags of free merchandise.

April 2020

Due to a global pandemic, the Distillery and outlet shop are shut till further notice.

September 2020

Accountants for Water Horse Distillery are very concerned about the liquidity situation of the Company.

Prentis smooths things over, eventually.

October 2020

Weebeeny dies of a heart attack.

Aimee is distraught and immediately arranges a pet funeral with much-lovedpets.com

The funeral costs £5,000 due to the volume of flowers and a pet-loving humanist fee for taking the service.

The pet cemetery is tastefully located in the corner of a cow field.

Aimee remains off work indefinitely due to her bereavement.

November 2020

Prentis sacks all five Polish employees for incompetence and suspected theft, despite lack of any evidence. He is getting more stressed these days.

Amazon.uk sells some single malts from the distillery at £20 a bottle. People rush to buy!

Harrods do not order anymore gin.

Prentis mixes older stock of better whisky with younger, inferior cask stuff and bottles it as a non-age statement version for the category.

Online 'Influencers' receive free bottles of rum and whisky through the post and a few of them rave about the brand, then ask for more samples . . . but sales continue to decline.

December 2020

Sales are very poor for this time of year.

New employees are not settling into the Distillery.

Prentis has a long, much needed chat with Sheryl his wife.

Prentis asks his lawyer for advice, and a private investigator is commissioned to investigate Piers Bally-Winser.

March 2021

The investigator hired by Prentis's lawyers submits a report highlighting a few things:

- Piers has a long-term cocaine habit, and has significant gambling debts,

- He changed his name by deed poll in 2005 from Bertrand Jones to his current name.

- Arrest for alleged attempted rape in 2006.

- Arrest for alleged attempted extortion in 2007.

- At least five failed business partnerships in the U.K. due to his misappropriation of assets and collateral.

April 2021

Prentis shuts Water Horse Distillery for good, and closes down his Company.

The stock market has collapsed, and there is now a serious international economic recession.

On discovering that Piers has sold all the casks owned by PiersPrentis Ltd, about five times over to different 'cask investors', he attempts to close down PiersPrentis. Ltd.

Debts of this Company now stand at £6.000.000.

Prentis tries to phone Piers, but calls are not answered. He loses patience after only one day and gets his lawyers to step in and sort out the problem.

May 2021

The global drinks Industry goes onto a steep downturn due to changing drinking habits amongst the younger generation, along with increased regional regulation and international government bureaucracy.

People no longer have the money to spend due to rapid inflation and long-term economic uncertainty.

Age statements suddenly re-appear on whisky bottles as a 'dynamic category innovation', and marketing departments are given bigger budgets. The new Industry-agreed promotional buzz is 'brand integrity' and 'loving our life-styles'.

Things get worse quickly, and sales continue to decline.

Loyal and experienced customers continue to complain about poor quality bottlings.

August 2021

Corry and Cammy return from mainland Europe where they have been helping with the seasonal grape harvest and assisting with maintenance jobs at Italian vineyards.

They are older and wiser and now ready to do something back home.

September 2021

Corry is making custom beer for a bar in Finnieston, in a converted garage out the back at the licenced premises in the Hidden Lane, off Argyle Street.

Cammy is the bar tender there and they are both helping out an old friend from university who has recently converted the premises from a run-down liquor store which has recently gone bust. They are across from a funeral director which has never been busier than now due to the recession and its consequences.

Both Corry and Cammy are feeling very positive with recent developments and they admire their friends courage to risk starting a business at such a bad time in the economy.

He makes it clear that he can't pay much but will split the profits evenly with all employees.

They are clearly motivated to make things work, and they do.

The bar is busy weekday afternoons with traditional pub lunches, and a book club meets every Tuesday for 'afternoon tea and readings'. In the evening, music students from the local college busk and gig for the cavalcade of customers who love the vibe.

The place is considered 'sick', 'cool' and is always busy.

October 2021

The Bar is expanded into the next commercial unit and a 'Food&Drink Club' is formed, modelled on the style of a traditional delicatessen. Soon, the place is getting even busier.

Corry starts a 'brewing club' where people can brew their own beers and ales under supervision.

Cammy extends this to include 'distillery school' where he distils for customers according to their needs.

The bar and deli combination breaks even within three years and will make modest profits by the fourth year.

November 2021

Prentis visits Corry and Cammy to show them his O.B.E. medal. It sits in a flat, modest box with a Maltese cross appearance topped by a red ribbon. Prentis is very proud that Princess Ann gave him the medal at a short ceremony within the grounds of Holyrood House in Edinburgh.

Corry and Cammy are polite but disinterested.

Prentis sees that they are busy and leaves shortly after showing them his award.

He is busy himself, having recently sold his home and stables in the countryside to downsize into a three bedroom flat in Falkirk. Sheryl is not happy, but she is busy arranging Aimee's wedding to a local businessman near where they live. It will be an expensive affair.

December 2021

After laying low in South Africa for a year, Piers Bally-Winser, who is now called Berty Bellinghem, is provided with a fresh start as an executive in a British N.G.O. Charity, which encourages and supports young children in rural parts of the Gambia to express themselves with sport and performance art. He is based in Serrekunda just south of Banjul where he keeps Whitehall informed of paedophile activities, and as a result is well rewarded with a salary of £120,000 a year.

His main task is to supervise the distribution of bribes to local government officials.

January 2022

Early edition bottles of Water Horse whisky and rum are now considered 'collectable' bottles at auctions, where the prices have doubled in the last three months. Scarcity and quality of content seem to be the key to this acquired status, especially to the bottles signed by Corry and Cammy.

March 2022

Corry and Cammy win 'Innovative Distillers of the Year 2022' at a National Drinks Event, and demand for their brand grows so quickly that any public investment is by invitation only, and strictly on their own terms. People rush to try and invest.

Friday in Tinseltown.

- a City, a Street, a Pub, another day.

A cold north wind blows hard across the slated roof tops of Charing Cross in Glasgow, driving the autumnal chill within it, and hurling down rain onto roads and pavements beneath. As the descending rain meets the sodium glow of street lighting, the air sparkles with the broken light animating the wet drops which spangle and glitter within the turbulence of the elements.

Cars start and stop as green lights turn to red, and people rush and push along, with umbrellas slowly disintegrating from the violent turbulences of air and water. Some are going home, some going nowhere, some going out, for a meal, for a drink, for a conversation, for a laugh. All is as it usually is and should be, within the warm heart of this cold City. It is Friday in Tinseltown.

The Bon Accord, just down the road from Charing Cross, has been open since ten o'clock in the morning, and in the quiet of the first few hours, the long dark oak counter has been polished and re-arranged, removing any over-looked damp beer mats and dried out glass rings, left from the night before.

Toilets are cleaned, tables wiped, and the cellar has been checked, with the beer lines leading to the floor above carefully cleaned and rinsed if required.

As the best whisky bar in Britain, the Bon Accord has a reputation which it successfully protects as a small family business, with the vocation of the licensed trade in its blood.

The tall, dark, and sturdy wooden gantry behind the bar shimmers with illuminated bottles of whisky, about four hundred in total, which compliments the range of guest beers and ales which amount to a rolling turnover of eight hundred different brands a year.

It is a busy place. Welcoming, understated and accommodating of customers who arrive, looking for a better bar experience.

Thomas, . . .tall, dark-haired, broad-framed, and the heir to the business, stomps up the steps from the basement and emerges into the foyer at the back door, glancing, briefly left towards the smell of cooking and food prep where all is familiar and organised. At the bar he chats with his two assistants who tell him about the calls he's missed from reps, brand ambassadors and other on-trade salespeople.

By half past ten, the first customers arrive through the green painted front door, its brass hinges creaking softly, alerting staff to their presence.

Some Japanese tourists arrive wearing freshly wetted waterproofs and walking boots, curious and wanting the real scotch bar experience. They stay for an hour before departing to get the train from Queen Street railway station to Edinburgh, and as they leave, they seem happy with the start to their first day in Scotland.

Two old pals shuffle in from the rain, Billy, and Bobby, in town for a day out from Summerston.

The two fellas are retired janitors who worked together for about thirty years at Springburn Academy before jointly accepting an early retirement package.

They have done quite well out of it and are glad to get away from the daily grind of diluted warm bleach, childrens' predictable stupidity and cheek, and the complaints of bossy, moaning, exasperated teachers. With the budget they have, a once-a-week day trip into the city centre, with a drink and a pub lunch is an affordable treat. Getting into the Kelvingrove Art Galleries and Transport Museum for free is also a bonus, and their saltire travel card allows them to go on the underground train cheaply.

Billy, who is better with cash, orders up the two pints of 'Old Fruity Harvest' and after scanning the bottles arrayed across the gantry, adds a couple of glasses of house blend scotch to his bill.

They sit by the front window, not saying much, as they know each other too well not to be bothered by some extra silence.

Ross, young, serious, and with swept back short dark hair, sticks his head through the door, "Has Sandy been in yet?" he asks, as bar staff wag their heads negatively back across the space between them.

"Oh! Well, maybe later," he says, then turns back out into the rain lashing down North Street.

One minute later, Sandy walks confidently though the door ready for his first beer and a chaser.

With short light hair and an affable disposition, the ambient and animated buzz of soft intoxication is his happy space, and the Bon Accord is a magnet to the metal of his daily routine.

He has a sedentary job, not one that means a lot to him, it pays the bills, and pays for the drink along with the passing company of friends and strangers, whilst the opportunity for people-watching in his local haunt comes free of charge.

Sandy wants to run his own brewery, however, the dream remains a dream, and he seems content to let the dream continue within the thought-loop of his unfulfilled ambitions.

The back door opens and a tall, white-haired, red-faced man ambles into the premises with the passive awareness of one who knows the venue well.

Paul the proprietor pauses to stick his head into the kitchen and say good morning to the catering team before heading along and up a few steps to the end of the bar. He glances carefully around, looking for anything out of place or unfamiliar, but all is as it should be, so he turns his attention to his son who hands him a short list of phone messages.

They chat and laugh a little over whisky matters, trade gossip, and brewery situations, then, finally to family matters, which are, of course, the most important.

A small, slight, silver-haired, and academic looking man appears, pausing, waiting silently and patiently for recognition. Henrik is from Sweden, and as business has been concluded early at his employers office in Bath Street, he is taking the moment to have a beer and whisky, before being uplifted by the taxi he has pre-booked, to take him to the airport. A fussy, nervous man, outwardly timid, and totally unassuming, his specialist software experience has made him valuable to his employers, so they reward him well.

He orders a Deuchars I.P.A. and as the pint is slowly poured, he scans the length of the gantry from side to side, and then side to side again, and after pausing briefly as if to consider the potential cost, he tentatively asks how much the Ardbeg Lord Of The Isles 25yo malt is!

"Fifty-five pounds!" responds Thomas, lifting over the bottle for closer inspection by his customer.

"And that's for thirty-five mil:" he adds reassuringly.

Henrik nods his consent, and for sixty more minutes, until his taxi toots its horn briefly outside on the street, he is content, and engaged in the ambient illumination of the bar, enhanced by the soft bitterness of his fresh beer, intertwined with the unfolding peat-complex, wood-infused charisma of a classic Scottish Islay single malt.

Jerry and Norrie crash in through the door, still roaring with laughter about the beer club novice who admitted, under the influence of drink, and at a club night after a bit of prompting, that his fifty bottles of fresh-made, home-bottled beer had started exploding in the heat of a garden shed. The neighbours complained about the bangs, the fizzing, the smell of unripe ale, and the swarm of flies that descended onto, and around the mess. The lad could not get in till about midnight to throw a duvet over the remaining intact bottles, and thus, reduce the risk of broken bottle glass flying out and across the garden.

The boys grandmother was not very pleased either, it was her shed, but, it could have been worse, as he had originally planned to do his inaugural, and discreet brewing in her green house.

Norrie is more sympathetic, after all, we all make mistakes, and what beer enthusiast has never had an 'incident'. Jerry is not so charitable, after all, the boy had not listened to advice, and was in too much of a rush, these lads are always in such a bloomin' rush.

Like a couple of oversized garden gnomes, they linger at the bar, as a young lady waits patiently, and engagingly for their order. They are in no rush, scrutinising each, and every option of cask conditioned ale.

Eventually, she chips-in some guidance, "The 'Moaning-Molly' is just on, won a rosette at the CAMRA meet last month," she states, pauses, then adds, "Citra hops and optic barley."

They look at one another for approval, then back to their bar attendant, positively nodding their consent. Soon, the validation of the choice is evident in their quiet murmurs of pleasure as they take a seat for more gossip and a laugh in the corner by the window, facing the bar so that they can see what other customers are buying then comment to each other about it, and have a laugh.

Next to them is an academic looking Scandinavian with an empty glass of beer and a, soon-to-be finished, glass of peaty, oak-infused whisky. The beer fans can tell by the smell that it's good stuff, and probably expensive too.

They nod their silent approval to the quiet man beside them when he catches their eyes lingering briefly upon him, and after a short while, he gets up and leaves in response to a toot from a vehicle outside on the road waiting to take him somewhere else.

The two beer-chums continue an intense conversation about the cavalier barley variety being re-introduced from the 'seed bank' and how it's enzymic levels may be too high, or too low for current brewing innovations.

They are so engrossed within the subject that they fail to notice the lunch-time customers arriving at the bar and ordering drink and food.

Amongst them are Hugh and Jamil, both down from the Mitchell Library, and despite being only a few hundred yards in walking distance, they are soaking wet from a sudden additional heavy downpour of rain.

Hugh is chubby, with a look of a domesticated mummy's boy, a complete mischaracterisation which often leads to misunderstandings.

They shake down their wet coats and claim a reserved table tucked away at the back of the seating area, underneath an oversized television screen with vividly coloured sports coverage, and on mute.

"Well that's going to kick off a shit-storm," declares Hugh to his friend.

"I never expected this much drama and skulduggery from book collectors," responds Jamil.

"Never seen anything like this, the money, the cunning, the gullibility."

They pause to order food and a couple of Glenfarclas, the 15yo, as it's a bit stronger, and nicely sherried.

With the Glencairn glasses now in front of them, and the bar lady off taking another order at another table, they lower their voices and discuss the assignment they have been working on.

Slim, bespectacled and of a pale, academic earnestness, off-set by a mop of dark wavy hair, Jamil is unimposing and, some would say, dull to behold.

His job is certainly not dull, and it takes him book-searching and literary treasure hunting all around the World. He is a manuscript detective.

His latest commission is undoubtedly his most lucrative and his most challenging.

"You see Hughy, I really was confused as to how such a known valuable book could get past scrutiny and not be nailed as a fake." frowns Jamil.

"It just suddenly appeared in Australia last year from a dealer in Melbourne, selling on behalf of a known antiquarian. Audubon's 'The Birds Of America', first 'Havell' edition, circa 1828," he pauses reflecting, "As you know, the last public sale was in 2012 where a copy went for over eight million, and as we all know, it's the go-to money maker in rare books, despite its visibility.

I'm not aware of any private sales recently, but this one has been weird from the moment it appeared."

"Yes!" affirms Hugh, "We did the forensics, and even with the Libraries limited resources, we noticed it to be fake. The colours are too fresh, the condition too perfect. So when we saw the analysis sample was genuine, it was reasoned that an original sliced print was inserted into the pages of the fake book to provide for sound chemical sampling, but I tell you what Jamil, they did a bloody good job, the fake looks way better than any original."

He stops, suddenly, looking puzzled. "Are good fakes the new genuine?" he asks.

They pause to sip their whiskies, splashing in a little water waiting patiently in a compact glass jug behind their glasses.

"And..." continues Hugh, "Tell me more!".

Two super-rich Chinese business men have had a fall-out over a building project." whispers Jamil, "And one wants revenge, so the book has been a sting, and as he has a printing operation, he also has the technology to recreate old originals to a better standard than ever thought possible, even a few years ago."

Jamil brings out some folded prints of magnified photo images, "Just look at the quality of the ink splatter, . . . it's amazing!" then he moves to another picture, "And look at the paper, no fluro-chems in it, the best reproduction of antique paper I have ever seen, the patina, the digital ageing, the precise discolouration . . . this is state-of-the-art!"

They look at one another as the scale of the deception continues to unfold.

"I find out that the fake has been constructed from nano-scans on location off an original edition lent by a businessman in Qatar as part of a transportation deal."

"The quality is superb, just superb, the best I have ever seen, . . . but!" he continues looking intently at Hugh, "There were particles of dust embedded in the binding glue, only found in China, and nowhere else."

The two investigators look up to see their fish and chips arriving, and swiftly conclude the subject of conversation.

"So how much did he pay for it then?" asks Hugh.

"When he found out his rival wanted it, he upped to twenty-two million!"

"U.S. dollars?" asks Hugh,

"Aussie dollars," replies Jamil,

"Now he's suing for forty million."

Hugh shakes his head, and they both eat their fish and chips, with another round of the Glenfarclas for afters.

Across the restaurant area, at a larger table three young men, still in their early twenties, are sitting, joking, laughing, and enjoying some insult-banter.

They are Rufty, Tufty and Drippy, three rough-edged amigos, who have known each other since primary school days in Maryhill. They have just eaten burgers, better quality, and far better value than the big brand corporates out on the high street, and they sit contentedly with three glasses of Springbank 12yo cask edition, 2016 vintage.

Casually dressed in cheap branded sports clothes, they look rather out of place, except for the confident nature of their conversation, and ease of mood, due to successful careers and good money.

The conversation is light, cheeky and good humoured.

"So ya wee shite!" states Tufty, "How did you do it then?" he demands to know of his younger, slimmer friend, a tall, dark-haired, shyly unassuming, and seemingly naive young man.

Drippy blushes, and flashes a grin at the other two, looking away suddenly as they are now displaying hints of amicable jealousy.

"Just winged it really, never thought too much, 'cos the more you think, the more they see your mind and your moves," he concludes.

"But three hundred grand in one night!" exclaims the taller, bespectacled Rufty.

Drippy's silence confirms the scale of his professional poker prize money win.

"It takes me a whole year to earn that sort of money at NorthOrbital." declares Rufty.

The red-haired Tufty nods in agreement with his pal, "All these hours we put in on game engine programming." He shakes his head in disbelief and admiration.

"How much is that you've won now, this year. . . so far?" demands Rufty, pushing his glasses back up on his nose.

About, sort-of, well. . . over half a million anyway, enough to let my mum buy her house and save a fortune on rent. . . and then some."

Rufty and Tufty look across the table at each other, whilst Drippy takes in the silence of their admiration.

"You're nothin' but a skelf, mate, a wee skinny ned, and yet . . ." muses Tufty,

"You leave school to work in the local supermarket and end up as a ranked poker player on the International circuit," muses Rufty.

"You couldna' script it fur' fucks sake," concludes Tufty in admiration.

"So where's our celebration malts, mate?"

As Drippy shuffles up the steps to the bar to order three more glasses of Springbank, his two friends look at one another for a moment in silence.

"He's doing well for himself," states Tufty.

"We all are," replies Rufty, appreciatively.

"We got lucky when we gave luck a helping hand," he concludes.

They soon finish the fresh malts, and head off out into the rain to find a taxi to take them down to the PlayExpo at the Braehead Arena, where they are meeting gamers, hosting a Q&A., Instabling-ing, twittering, and being adored by fans.

As they leave, one of the two loudly dressed, and expensively manicured older ladies at the table next to them explodes with a shriek of laughter.

"Am telling you Ella," says Ruby, "Am just tellin' you that you can't knock it till you try it!"

Ella smiles back across the table, disinterested in her friends recollections of having regular sex with a local man forty years her junior, whilst staying at the Tropics Montego Bay Eco Village in Jamaica, just the previous week.

Ruby is still gushing with enthusiasm from the experience.

Having recently become a widow, after her husband passed away from a mystery illness, Ruby has now been living her fantasies for real, guided by her recently discovered friend Ella, who, having had a similar situation herself several years ago, has provided comfort and support.

They are having a shopping day and have popped in for a light lunch before heading off to the West End for coffee and a people-watch.

Ella appears slightly remote and uninterested, but Ruby does not seem to notice, so she tells some more of her adventure.

"So, I'm just tellin' you darlin, he was such a gentleman, and a big boy too, and I mean", she winks, "Big."

"Lovely apartment, lovely tropical colours and wee palm trees, in wee pots, all over the place, and, Bentley, that's his name, you know, Bentley who is from an ancient local family, who, like, worked in sugar plantations and smuggling, and lead an uprising, well, he, was, you know, well, just such a good listener, and when we were at it, for hours and hours, you know, well, he played with himself when I stopped for a smoke, and I needed another smoke, and anyway, cigarettes are so cheap out there, and it's so sunny, and the reggae music too, you know, we danced all night then smoked weed too, it was c-r-a-z-y, like."

She pauses.

"I think we have some chemistry Ella."

"What do you think Ella darling?" she adds.

Ella does not respond.

"So, you know, . . . I paid him well for his company, but I think we actually have a wee spark of something more."

Ruby pauses again to better judge Ella's reaction.

"He's coming over to London next month to open a wee ReggaeRhythm Restaurant in Soho, and I am going to be the manager, and, well, it's like, Ella, it's like a dream coming true, and, were going to be together once more."

"If he's Bentley, I should change my name to Ferrari," she shrieks again with laughter.

Ella glances sharply across at her friends latest unexpected disclosure, and then looks away.

She thinks of herself, and an old friend called Patsy, and of Annabel, and now of Ruby, and she feels the cold chill of something dying again inside of her which she cannot quite explain.

"Another gin and tonic Ruby?" she asks. "On me. . . my treat."

"Oh yes please Ella, and could you make it a double?"

"My pleasure sweetheart," responds Ella smiling, and heads briskly towards the bar, looking out a small bottle of white tablets from within her handbag.

By two o'clock in the afternoon, the place quietens down as lunchers return to their workplace, or to the shops that they have still to shop in.

A few regulars remain, enjoying the quiet, the detachment, and the warm shelter from the cold and rain outside.

Paul has been in the office at the back, a small, yellow-lit inadequate space, crowded with files, and papers, and bills, and bottles. Now bored with the piles of paperwork, he heads back out into the bar to get a coffee.

After a check with Thomas at the bar he wanders outside for a smoke and a look-see, holding open the door to allow two more customers to enter the premises.

The two pleasant Rastafarian-looking chaps acknowledge his consideration with a nod and smiles, and amble over to the bar for some refreshment. Rudy and Dennis have just arrived off the train from Wemyss Bay for a concert tonight at the Barrowlands Ballroom over at the Trongate, just by Glasgow Cross, and it's a great venue for a good night out and the atmosphere will be 'wickid'.

Damian Marley is playing with his band, and the rumour is that Bunny Wailer might make a guest appearance later on, . . . now that would be something special.

The two friends have also noticed that there will be a Rum and Reggae night later in the year, and they are excited to have got tickets for that event too.

Rudy orders two carlings and two house rums, and they seem well impressed with the quality of the rum, it's Caroni 18yo cask strength, and delicious, even though Dennis thinks they can make better stuff at home, given enough time. Rudy agrees, but he's not sure if it will be better stuff.

They sit down at the front door next to two older chaps who have entered before them and are making the most of the mid-afternoon quiet for an intense chat about old Clyde puffer boats.

Bobby and Edward have not known each other for very long.

They met recently at a restorer's meeting for an old, derelict puffer, donated to the enthusiasts by an Irish businessman, looking to clear an old dock on the coast at Ballymena for redevelopment.

The 'Skye Mist' is in a sorry state, but still sea-worthy and is being towed by tug up to Bowling for a complete restoration.

With the success of the Vic 52 puffer, which is now operating as a charity and offering holidays to puffer fans, the extended team of volunteers are relishing the new project.

Bobby has bought the drinks, two pints of 'Anchor I.P.A.' and two glasses of Bunnahabhain 12yo.

"I hear you were in the Navy Bobby!", declares Edward.

"What, me, never, never been to sea until I got roped into helping out on building the reception centre at Crinan. I've been a builder all my life, until I retired a while back, and after I sorted a few problems out, moved into a rented flat belonging to a work-mate, . . . then got a bit stir-crazy."

"And yourself Edward, what's your story?"

Edward looks misty-eyed for a moment, as if suddenly engulfed by memories and histories.

"Well, I started out in life as a deck-hand on an old boat, a puffer, called the 'Kelpie'. I was only about twelve, but the crew were kind enough, although the Captain was past-it for sure, must've been in his eighties, but just could not retire, I don't think he had any money saved."

Edward pauses again to think a little deeper.

"Captain Nimmo, I'm sure that was his name, quiet old chap, not like the first mate who caused trouble whenever he could."

"The engineer kept the peace, he was a fine character, got me a job with CalMac after the puffer was left beached at Stornoway Bay, then left to rot."

He smiles at the memory, "You know Bobby, mate, when I first boarded the Vic 52 last year, it all came back to me, suddenly, as if that old boat was just waiting to remind me!".

"They were far simpler times, I can tell you." he concludes, then downs his Bunnahabhain in two swigs of the glass. "Oh!, that was just nice." he exclaims, "I once spent a night sleeping on the floor at that distillery, really uncomfortable, so thank goodness I was pished at the time!"

Bobby is slower to finish his dram, but as soon as he is done, the two men put their raincoats back on, and head off outside for a passing bus to take them to the Transport Museum along the road at Finnieston. As they leave, Paul holds the door open to allow them to exit into the rain and wind, and then things go quiet for an hour or so, until the bar re-animates just after five o'clock with commuters and early-revellers.

At six o'clock, some young ladies, inadequately dressed for the climate, pull open the door, look inside, see it's an 'old' place, and then swiftly depart, chattering loudly, and heading up North Street tottering along on their high heels and with their Instagram updates, towards Sauchiehall Street, where the crowd is younger, noisier and with less to talk about.

When the door opens next, a few minutes later, two overweight gentlemen in golf slacks cautiously manoeuvre into the seats nearest the door, and Benny turns to Barry, his friend, and asks for a lager. Barry asks if Benny wants a whisky, a malt, of course.

Benny confirms, swiftly, that the Carlsberg will do. . . and not to bother with a whisky.

"Oh, go on mate, it's my round." exclaims Barry, trying to curry favour with his friend, who nearly abandoned him after a recent embarrassment at their exclusive whisky club.

"Oh, all right then, what have they got?" chuckles Benny.

Barry peers across the bar, ignoring the staff as if they are invisible,

"Oh!" he declares, "They seem to have rather a lot of choices."

Benny quickly gets up from the table, scattering his scarf across the seat to make it look more occupied.

It is several minutes later, and Benny has just been handed a bottle of sixty year old Glenlivet to look at. As soon as he has established how much it costs for a bottle from his mobile app, he asks for a glass of house malt, keeping the valuable bottle sitting on the bar where he can photograph it.

Barry is summoned back to take the picture from the table where he has just been pouring two glasses of Carlsberg from bottles.

Benny holds the glass of house malt aloft, smiling knowingly, with the sixty year old Glenlivet bottle strategically placed on the bar to be most visible within the picture.

Benny thanks the barmaid, and the two resume their seats.

"Not as rough as I expected," chuckles Benny, tapping quickly into his Instagram post message and messaging, "Age and quality is always worth the premium, just like me !", underneath the image of himself with the Glenlivet.

He quickly gets positive responses as his blog channel 'Whiskymaltmaestro.com' is starting to grow, as is his Twitter account.

Already, Water Horse Distillery are sending him their bottlings for reviews and courting him as an 'ambassador'. His reviews are glowing, especially for the non-age statement stuff in the 50cc bottles.

He has had an amber-coloured card printed, -

Benny Benbow Esq:

Whisky Consultant

'turning water into gold'

#whiskymaltmaestro

He has just handed one of his cards to the barmaid, who accepts it graciously and quickly puts it out the way under the till.

Barry quickly becomes jollier as the atmosphere is quite relaxing, unlike the Whisky Circle Club that they both belong to, and where Barry, especially never feels quite at ease.

He heads back up to the bar for a second round of Carlsberg's, and feeling jovial, offers to recite a limerick to the barmaid.

She seems bewildered at first with such an offer from a rather expensively dressed man but agrees out of curiosity.

He begins:

"There was a young man called MacNair,

who made love to his wife on the stair,

when the bannister broke . . .

. . . without missing a stroke,

he finished her off in mid-air"

"Boom Boom!"

"Barry, you stupid idiot," bellows Benny from the table.

The still-giggling barmaid swifty departs up the bar to the till.

"What the hell do you think you're doing, have you learned nothing you oaf, we have a status to consider, and I think that bottle of chianti at the Rogano this afternoon has clouded your judgement, . . . idiot."

Benny is not pleased.

"I insist you go and apologise at once to the staff!" he demands.

But just as Barry goes to rise, the front door opens and a middle-aged, bespectacled workman in a tartan fleece ambles in, wearing a singular tweed cap.

"Oh my god!" gasps Benny, dragging Barry back down into his seat.

"Don't look, don't look, . . . it's that prick Ralfy, oh my god, what a total arsehole, and what's he doing here?"

"Have you seen his videos?" he hisses, shaking his head side to side,

" . . . Just a load of rubbish, and full of opinions and such, quite unwatchable, I just don't know how he gets any attention at all, he's simply not the right sort, and he doesn't know his place, its awful!"

Barry remains silent, registering the distress in Benny's voice.

"My good pal, Sammy," continues Benny, "Who used to have a proper review site, says he's just an upstart and a gobby prick, what with criticising the Industry and making stupid suggestions for improvements, honestly, who the FUCK does he think he is?" blasts Benny, now shivering with rage. After a few minutes of observation, Benny continues, "He is supposed to have written a silly little book, full of spelling errors with a weird story in it about greeks getting drunk on a hill, and I heard that it's got a secret code in it and contains a message about the location of a very rare Port Ellen, hidden somewhere in a distillery building, . . somewhere!"

Ralfy is now at the bar, shaking hands with the publican Paul, and waving cheerily to the staff down at the till.

Thomas strides up past the gantry, "Ralfy! How you doin' my man?" adding, "Long time no see!"

Ralfy grins back, "Busy, Thomas, always busy, somewhere out in the Irish Sea, in the Bothy, fightin' off the pirates and hiding the stash from smugglers."

He adds, "Can I have a pint of something crispy please, and some water for Orlando the cat?"

A ginger cat is now sitting patiently on top of a dry beer mat next to the ale pumps.

It seems oddly out of place but is ignored by the customers.

"You see," sniffs Benny to Barry, as they both earwig the conversation above them, "He's just a wee mouthy gob-shite with delusions of grandeur and such, no class at all . . . he's not like us!"

They both get up noisily, and leave, with Benny casting a backwards nasty look towards the people at the bar, now engaged in updates and catch-ups.

Paul is telling Ralfy about the temporary exhibition at the Hunterian Museum at Glasgow University.

A historic illegal distilling operation has recently been discovered near a stream above Loch Arklett, up by Loch Lomond, and with so much of the relics intact, a team of archaeologists has examined and documented an almost full inventory of a nineteenth century hidden building with distilling equipment, everything was present except the casks they would have stored their liquor in.

Ralfy listens intently and agrees to make time to go and view the exhibition as soon as he can, and as the university is near to Byres Road, it will be a good day out, seeing both the exhibits in the museum, and also down on Byres Road, where the west-end eccentrics strut their entertainingly delusional and pretentious life-styles in a faux bohemian haze.

The subject of conversation changes, just as two young lovers wander in, out of the rain. They order drinks and take a seat, a soda and lime for Weezil, and a gin and a Dubonet for his girlfriend Somi.

They find a table in the corner by the front window, out of the way and beneath a bright display cabinet of exotic, expensive looking bottles. Having secured their drinks, they sit silently, saying nothing, . . . just watching the people and the place.

Ralfy is chatting to both Paul and Thomas about Bonneville, the adventure, the challenge, the success of achieving a world land-speed record in 2016. It's an interesting tale of long-odds and strange twists. It is the tale of 'Salty Wheels' They have heard it before but want to hear it again.

"I'm going back there Paul, sometime" says Ralfy, grinning, "To help another team, and to enjoy the uniqueness, the machines, the salt. . . without the pressure of being a rider."

Paul nods knowingly, adding "Do you want the pub to sponsor you again, and I'm sure Tam at scotchwhiskyauctions would be keen to back you after the last success, and that amazing bottling to celebrate it."

"Thanks Paul," replies Ralfy, "Much appreciated mate."

"By the way," asks Paul, "Have you tried the new Water Horse Distillery bottlings?"

"No!" replies Ralfy, ". . . Not on my List!"

The bar is very busy now, lots of people consuming lots of drinks.

Suddenly, the bar seems to notice developments at the table in the corner.

A small, skinny, dark-haired young man has dropped a small hard gift box, and it clatters across the floor,

Ralfy stoops to pick it up and deliver it back to the blushing, and clearly awkward lad.

The lady with him blushes too and grins, briefly covering her face with her hands.

Weezil pauses, hesitating to open the small box.

Somi, steps in,

"Do I love you?

Yes, I love you!

Will we always be so happy go lucky?"

There is a pause.

". . . just give me the damn ring, murakha!" she laughs.

Weezil leans across the table and lets Somi slip the small, glittering ring over her finger.

As they both hold hands, the bar around erupts with loud cheering and clapping.

Paul the proprietor steps across and says that he will fix them up with their next drinks, and Ralfy comes across to shake their hands before departing off out into the cold, dark and wet.

He strides briskly down North Street to the junction with Argyle Street, where it is usually sound for picking up a taxi heading back into the city centre. As he waits, he lifts his head to feel the rain again, and he feels the music of Tinseltown. Tinseltown in the rain, a spangle and a shimmer of life, an energy resilient to poverty and neglect.

Cars stop and start as red lights turn to green, and people push and rush along with umbrellas slowly disintegrating. . . and he laughs aloud in the busy street,

because,

hey!

. . . there's a red car in the fountain.

Epilogue

I do hope that you have enjoyed reading these diverse stories which I have picked up over the years from conversations in bars and from whisky clubs.

Whisky, and other quality spirits, are always accompanied by drama and the diversity of human experience.

Please feel free to follow me on my YouTube.com Channel 'ralfydotcom', and 'fitterphilosophy' where I provide weekly updates of content and opinion.

And remember malt-mates, keep it quality, not quantity.

My First book 'Search For A Whisky Bothy' is available to buy on all good online book retailers.

Made in the USA
Monee, IL
30 November 2022